Findii

Sarah Louise Smith

jandsromance.co.uk

Praise for Sarah Louise Smith's other books:

"A hidden gem... she really should be up there with Sophie Kinsella & Marian Keyes. Just a perfect read."

~

"A laugh out loud, lump in your throat, heart pounding roller-coaster."

~

"An uplifting story full of will-they-won't-they twists and turns, gorgeous locations, great characters and delicious romance."

~

"From the minute you pick this up you are thrown into a whirlwind of devastation, a hurricane of love and drama. It's fabulous."

~

"I was engrossed pretty much immediately.
I fell asleep with my kindle in my hand and almost as soon as I woke up, I had switched it on again to carry on reading...
The characters are so beautifully created that it feels real."

Copyright

First published by J&S Romance Ltd in 2024

Copyright © 2024 Sarah Louise Smith 2024

Sarah Louise Smith asserts the moral right to be identified as the author of this work.

This story is a work of fiction. All names, characters, and incidents portrayed in it are entirely from the author's imagination. Any resemblance to actual persons or events is entirely coincidental.

All rights reserved under International Copyright Conventions. No part of this publication may be reproduced, distributed, or transmitted in any form or by any means, including photocopying, recording, or other electronic or mechanical methods, without the prior written permission of J&S Romance Ltd.

About the Author

Sarah Louise Smith writes feel-good modern romance novels. She lives in a village in Northamptonshire, England and you'll often find her outdoors, hugging trees. She loves travelling to beautiful places, and in particular Scotland, the setting for this story.

Find out more at sarahlouisesmith.com and follow her on social media @iamsarahlsmith ~ she'd love to hear from you.

Sarah is also co-founder of J & S Romance, an independent book publisher.

Find out more about us at jandsromance.co.uk.

Also by Sarah Louise Smith:

The Only One For Me

Izzy's Cold Feet

The Truth About Ellen

Amy & Zach

Unrequited Alice

Independent Jenny

For Scotland

My Happy Place

My heart's in the Highlands,
my heart is not here,
My heart's in the Highlands,
a-chasing the deer;
Chasing the wild-deer,
and following the roe,
My heart's in the Highlands,
wherever I go.
~ Robert Burns

Marianne's Scottish Roadtrip

During this novel, Marianne travels all over Scotland, visiting many beautiful locations.

If you'd like to follow this route and see photos, or feel inspired to do a similar roadtrip, you can find all the information at:

sarahlouisesmith.com/mariannes-roadtrip

Chapter One

Marianne

I threw the last of my jumbled-up clothes, toiletries, and other essentials into my car, got into the driver's seat and set up the map for the first leg of my journey.

And... Deep breath.

Was I really going to do this? I looked out at the road in front of me and blinked a few times.

A road trip. Alone. Just me, my car, a bunch of clothes and other necessities... and the open road.

It both thrilled and terrified me.

I put some music on, put my foot on the accelerator. And I was off.

But maybe my story starts earlier. Maybe we need to go back a year, so you can understand why I, a sensible woman in her mid-thirties, would quit her job, leave her marriage, wave goodbye to her family and friends and go on a solo road trip, with no plans on what to do beyond that.

You see, I always wanted to be one of those women who had it all together. You know the type, the ones you see on social media in the beautiful house, living their 'best life', posting aesthetically pleasing photos every day.

I would bounce out of bed as soon as my alarm woke me up. Enjoy a 45-minute yoga workout before sipping my nutritious, homemade green smoothie. I'd have a seven-step skin-care routine that left me with glowing skin, only a dash of effortless makeup needed. Always manicured, pedicured and with a serene, happy sense of contentment about myself and how I looked.

I'd wear gorgeous clothes every day, with a real sense of smart-casual-chic style. Each morning I'd sashay to my car while waving good morning to the neighbours, carrying my healthy salad in one of those smart insulated lunch bags.

I'd be a confident, professional yet friendly lady-boss who got home in time to create a perfectly balanced meal for the family before sitting down to read an epic novel, glass of wine in hand, while listening to classical music. I'd still be full of energy come 9pm to make glorious, passionate love with my husband most nights (I'd say every night but that would perhaps be a little too unrealistic).

This version of me sleeps well, and is so organised that she always has enough time for friends, family, exercise, and hobbies. Life is balanced, healthy, calm, peaceful and yet also, fun.

Sadly, this version of me was completely fictional. In reality, I was a mess.

I muddled through life, with a forced smile. Until I hit crisis point.

It was only 7:30am on a Monday, and I'd already had a panic attack. The first time this had happened to me, I thought I was dying. The second; same. This time, I remembered the advice I'd read online; I just had to breathe through it. Easier said than done. It passed though, eventually, and I sat and stared at myself in the mirror for a while, wondering how I'd be able to function as a responsible adult if this kept happening.

There was no way I was going to be able to get anything done today, when I could feel the threat of another panic attack hanging over me. The thought of even dealing with work, or colleagues, or customers made me want to curl into a ball and sob. So, I made the inevitable phone call.

'I'm sorry Rich,' I lied. 'I've got a sickness bug. I was up all night and I feel terrible. Don't think I'll be able to come in today.'

It was the first time I'd ever lied to my boss. I did feel terrible, but my *stomach* was fine.

'No problem, Marianne,' he told me. I imagined him sitting at his desk, distracted by the 100's of emails that were always sitting in his mailbox. 'Take it easy, let me know how you are tomorrow.'

I spent the next two hours lying on the sofa in my pyjamas staring out at the magnolia tree in the garden, full of beautiful pink and white blossom, bouncing gently in the cool April breeze. I thought about going out there to smell the fragrant flowers, but it felt like too much effort. There was a pair of blue tits, flitting back and forth in the tree, then up to a bird feeder I'd topped up with peanuts. Then they'd pop to their little nest box that my husband, Ethan, had attached to the back wall. I envied them their freedom and simple life.

I recognised the signs; I'd been here before. Bleak thoughts. Low moods. Tears. Anxiety. As if those weren't bad enough, I now had a new problem with the panic attacks.

Some days, the best days really, I felt nothing at all; just numb. I went through this when I was sixteen, and my mother sent me to see a counsellor. I knew I was back in that dark place, and that I should speak to someone.

Ethan wouldn't really get it. Stoic and steady, he'd probably just ask if I was on my period or something. Nancy, my oldest and closest friend, would be supportive but we'd grown apart recently, she was a very busy mum of three little ones who had enough going on without me burdening her. My mum? She'd marched me to a counsellor the last time and thrown a load of classic novels at me. Mum loves literature: she says when you feel low, you should distract yourself in a world of wonderful fiction.

I didn't feel like reading.

I didn't feel like talking.

So, there I lay, staring out at the magnolia.

My stomach grumbled.

This wouldn't do. I should eat something. Get some water at the very least. I sat up, suddenly I had an idea. A feast. I could pull on some clothes, walk to the shop, grab all sorts of wonderful food, and be home again in less than twenty minutes.

So, that afternoon I stuffed my face full of calories while watching TV. I had a pre-packed sandwich, crisps, cakes, chocolate... I was halfway through a pack of chocolate chip cookies when I suddenly felt sick.

I tucked the remaining cookies away at the back of a cupboard. Then I cleared up the packaging, feeling ashamed and rather unwell. I hid the evidence as best I could in the bin, downed a litre of water and made myself a cup of peppermint tea, in the hope it'd help the nausea.

Ethan would be home in thirty minutes. I brushed my teeth so that he wouldn't be able to smell all that food on my breath. I got dressed. I sat at my desk, in the spare room. I often worked from home; and was usually shutting down my laptop when he came in.

'Hi Babe!' he called up the stairs.

'Hey!' I called back. I got up. My stomach felt like it might burst. I looked out of the window, at the magnolia again. I'd totally wasted my day, I realised. Tomorrow would be better, I'd make sure of it.

'What do you fancy for dinner?' Ethan was asking as I joined him in the kitchen.

I had two choices, as telling the truth was too shameful. I either went along with it and forced more food down; my stomach convulsed at the thought. Or I told him I felt sick.

'I'm not hungry. I'm feeling nauseous,' I told him. He closed the fridge and turned around, a look of concern across his handsome face. It was the truth, at least. How tragically ironic. I had self-inflicted nausea after telling my boss I had a sickness bug.

'Did you eat something that didn't agree with you?'

'I haven't eaten all day. Not felt good since breakfast.'

'That sucks,' he said, pulling me in for a hug. I wrapped my arms around my husband and yet I felt numb. I'd never lied to him before, and the dishonesty widened the already-growing distance between us, into more of a giant chasm.

'You're not...'

The unsaid word hung in mid-air, him hopeful, me trying not to roll my eyes.

'Pregnant? Nope, definitely not.'

I felt him deflate with disappointment as he kissed the top of my head. I decided not to point out that as we rarely had sex, it would be almost impossible. Let alone that I'd had a contraceptive coil fitted, which he seemed to have forgotten.

'Can I get you anything? Water? You need to hydrate.'

'Yes, please.'

As he stood at the sink letting my glass fill, I thought about our lack of intimacy.

I didn't feel like kissing him, let alone having sex. I didn't feel like doing anything I used to enjoy. I didn't feel like seeing friends, or doing any work, or even taking a shower.

I'd seen all the social media posts warning about depression, giving advice about what to do, suggesting ways out of the gloom. But I didn't have any desire to do anything about it.

I wanted to be enveloped in the dismal darkness. Wallowing was easier. I didn't want a solution. I would, I thought to myself, I would *try* to get better eventually. Probably. But not today.

'I think I'll just go to bed,' I told him as he handed me the glass.

I downed my water, got into bed, and stared up at the ceiling for a few hours. When Ethan came up, I closed my eyes and let my jaw drop a little, so it'd look like I was asleep. I listened to him tiptoeing around the room, felt him get into bed next to me, turn off his light. And then his breathing grew deeper, and I let out a few tears.

Numbness was better. This sadness was unbearable.

And the worst thing was, I didn't even know why.

I had the basics for happy living: a nice home, a nice husband, a nice job. I didn't love my work, but I didn't hate it either and I had nice colleagues. Nice isn't great, though. Or exceptional. I didn't feel challenged. I didn't have much fun. As for Ethan... something, somewhere, had been lost and I'd gone from feeling in love to feeling like I had a live-in friend. One who didn't even know or understand me that well.

Perhaps tomorrow I could set myself some goals. Plan something fun to look forward to.

Yet, I couldn't think of anything I'd like to do. A few more tears slipped down my face.

The silver lining: when Ethan left for work in the morning, I could eat the rest of those cookies for breakfast.

I didn't make any plans or set any goals so the binge-eating, magnolia staring day was repeated. Again. And again.

Two weeks later, Ethan was growing impatient. I'd managed to convince work I had some sort of terrible stomach virus. I even convinced my GP, who'd signed me off.

But Ethan saw past it. For one, I wasn't losing any weight. In fact, my pyjamas felt a little tight. And secondly, he'd not seen me rush to the bathroom once. Or take a shower. Or smile. I'd spent most of my time staring into space blankly, or crying, or sleeping.

'You've got to do something,' he said. 'Go for a walk. Do some yoga. Meditate. Play your piano. Watch TV, even.'

I just shrugged.

'Have you spoken to Nancy?'

I shook my head.

'Come on, Marianne. Don't just sit there staring at nothing.'

'I'm not staring at nothing,' I told him from the sofa. 'I'm admiring the magnolia.'

The blossom had gone, and bright green leaves were emerging. A reminder that nothing stays the same for long. That gave me just a little hope.

'What?' He went over to the window and looked out at the tree. 'Marianne, I'm worried about you.'

'I just feel a bit...'

'Bored,' he said, 'I know you're bored of work, bored of life, bored of our routine. Bored of me, no doubt.'

I didn't answer. He was right, I realised. I was lacking variety, fun and even romance.

'Come on, Marianne, do something, anything please!'

'I'll be okay,' I told him.

We kept having that same conversation, or variants of it. He just became more impatient, and I just became more stubborn.

Another two weeks after that, he opened the bedroom door one morning, and in walked Mum and Nancy. I started to cry, mostly out of embarrassment. My hair was greasy, I was in five-day-old pyjamas, and I'd been stuffing my face with crisps.

'Oh Marianne,' Mum said, wrapping one arm around me, while using the other to brush crumbs off my bed. Nancy hovered in the doorway beside Ethan, biting her lip. I didn't blame her; I wouldn't know how to handle me either.

'How about we get you washed and dressed?' Mum suggested, in her best condescending parent voice.

'I can do it myself,' I said, standing up. I realised I was shaking.

They waited for me in the living room. I agreed to see a counsellor. I forced a few smiles, and I saw them all glance at each other, relieved.

'How about a holiday?' Mum said, trying to find other ideas.

'You could go to Scotland!' Nancy said brightly. 'You've always wanted to go, and you got that scrapbook from your Grandad.'

'What's that?' Mum asked. She and Dad had been divorced for years. The book was from my dad's father.

'Grandad Tom gave me a travel journal when he went into the care home. It's got old photographs and descriptions of a month-long road trip he did with a friend. It's where he met my grandmother.'

'I remember your grandmother Nora talking about Scotland very fondly before she died. She was a lovely woman. You always said you wanted to go to Scotland when you were a kid,' Mum said, smiling. 'That's a great idea.'

'Nah,' Ethan swept away the flicker of enthusiasm that'd started to ignite within me for the first time in months. 'It's always raining in Scotland, I've zero interest in going there. How about somewhere sunny. Maybe the Canary Islands?'

'Oh lovely,' said Mum, grinning. 'Marianne, you'll love that.'

Nancy glanced at me, and I saw it in her eyes; she knew I'd prefer Scotland and she was sad for me that my husband didn't.

Mum and Ethan drifted off to the kitchen to make tea, talking about sunbeds and cocktails by the pool. He'd already got his iPad, and they started looking for deals.

I gazed around the room; with me being the way I had, nothing had been cleaned. Ethan had run the hoover round a few times but there was a thick layer of dust forming on every surface, including my beloved piano. I couldn't remember the last time I'd played.

'I'll come with you to Scotland,' Nancy said quietly, squeezing my hand. 'We could have a girly road trip.'

'Actually, I think I may do it on my own,' I told her, with no idea where the words had come from. I imagined visiting my grandad in the home, telling him I was finally going to go. He'd be chuffed to bits.

'Good for you! That'd be amazing. Life-affirming, I reckon.'

As I listened to Ethan and Mum comparing Canary Islands, I re-alised something.

I wasn't sure I wanted to be married anymore.

I made slow progress over the next few months with cognitive behavioural therapy. With the help of Sandra, Psychotherapist and Miracle Worker, I set little challenges for myself each week, and with great effort I started to do more; long walks, yoga, playing my piano, and reading. I went back to work. I began to feel just a little more like myself. Less depressed, less anxious. Less like staring at trees all day. The panic attacks came less often.

Sandra was kind, but firm. She didn't accept any whingeing, or victim mentality. She encouraged me to consider what I really wanted out of life.

I started to contemplate happiness. Perhaps, instead of some il-lusive concept that's brought about by chance, happiness is in fact something we can create. Something we can nurture. I'd been coasting through life, letting it happen to me, without contemplating what I really wanted, without setting any intentions, or taking any action to make it wonderful.

It was time to take life into my own hands, to shape my days, weeks, months, and years into a life I'd love, enjoy, and find fulfilling. This concept, the idea that I had control, made me feel frustrated that I'd not been living that way before, but also incredibly inspired. It was time to figure out what I wanted and make that my reality.

However, the better I felt, the bigger the chasm became between me and Ethan. I spent hours thinking about our relationship, and I talked to Sandra about it. I realised it'd been over a year since I'd really felt happy with our marriage. I *liked* him a lot, but I didn't feel romantic love towards him. Not even a little bit. I didn't understand what had changed or why, and it broke my heart.

Picking up on this perhaps, things between us grew more tense as the months went by. He was getting impatient about my mental health, wanting me to be 'cured' quickly. He kept dropping hints about having sex again, which I mostly ignored. He didn't understand why I wouldn't let him book a holiday to Tenerife. And he didn't understand why I couldn't 'pull myself together' faster.

During one argument, just a few weeks before Christmas, I reminded him of something.

'Doesn't *in sickness and in health* mean anything to you?' I asked.

'This started in spring! It's nearly Christmas!'

'And I've come a long way, but something still doesn't feel right.'

That something was him. Or, more accurately: Us. Our life together, our marriage. I was just too sad and too afraid to admit it out loud.

'What doesn't?' he said, his voice hard, and louder than necessary.

I shrugged. 'I've got mental health problems, Ethan.'

'This isn't poor mental health anymore Marianne, you can't compare being a miserable bitch to having a serious illness.'

And that, lovely reader, is when I finally told him I wanted to break up.

'You're just not yourself right now, this is crazy!' he said. 'You're having a midlife crisis.'

'At thirty-five, I'd say it was a bit early for that.'

'Is this about having a baby? Because I think it's time we talked about that.'

I sighed.

'I don't want kids, Ethan. I told you this before we got married, yet you keep dropping hints.'

'I thought you'd change your mind by now.'

'Well, I haven't.'

'You didn't tell me!' he raised his voice, unusual for him. I shook my head.

'Didn't tell you? I think it's safe to assume that if I don't tell you I've changed my mind, then I probably haven't. I made it clear from the start that I didn't want children.'

I knew I was right in this. I told him when we were dating, again when we got engaged and I made sure it was clear before we got married. I had never given any indication to the contrary.

The debate went long into the night. I told him we had drifted apart, that I didn't think he understood me. I said that I didn't want to go on package holidays or have children. I told him if he wanted those things, he needed to find someone who wanted them too. And eventually, he started to agree with me that we were on different paths. Things calmed down and we agreed to separate.

'It's just so very sad,' I said. We were both crying.

'It is,' he said, awkwardly putting an arm around me. 'I thought you were my forever person.'

'Me too, with you.'

After months of slowly getting better, feeling more myself, I felt so very sad again. We'd fallen in love with the dream of a happily ever after, and the thought of life without him was not only scary but heart-breaking. I didn't love him anymore, but I was grieving for the couple we once were. For the future I'd expected to have together, now shattered at our feet.

The next day, I packed my clothes and a few essentials neatly into bags. It felt like a weight had lifted, and despite the tears, I suddenly felt hopeful about my future for the first time in years. I dropped the stuff at my sister Jane's house. I rented a small storage unit and moved a bunch of other things out while Ethan was at work.

Our final goodbye came with an agreement that we should feel free to see other people right away. He suggested it. Didn't want to go without sex any longer, perhaps. I realised I didn't care if he met someone else, which was perhaps the saddest part of all.

I spent Christmas with my family. I tried to work out what I wanted as the new year started, and a few months passed. I stayed in Jane's spare room, no longer depressed but very confused. I didn't know what I wanted, only something different. And then, I realised. I wanted to go to Scotland. Not just for a short break. I wanted to take my time. I wanted to stare out at beautiful views for days on end, and figure out who I was.

I had been back at work for a good while, but I resigned a year to the day that I'd first called in sick. I worked my six weeks' notice. I had some savings and decided I was going to go to Scotland, for a month minimum, and just tour around, using my Grandad's journal as inspiration.

I needed to find Marianne. Not the wife, not the bored office work-er... but the real Marianne. Who was I, at my core? At a deep soul-level? I had no idea, but I was determined to find out.

A new home, a new career, a new me. But where, what, and how?

One thing I knew for sure; I wasn't falling in love again. It was too bloody painful when it ended. A few dates for fun – perhaps. Some sex – maybe. But love? No thanks.

So, back to the present, in my car, ready to leave. I pulled away from the curb, drove out of my hometown, and headed for the M6.

'*Scotland*,' I thought, '*I'm on my way. Please heal me. Please help me find myself again.*'

I hoped she was listening.

Chapter Two

Marianne

The journey so far had been good. I'd stopped a few times for a comfort break and took the time to get a coffee, rest, and then get back on the road. I listened to some interesting podcasts and time flew by.

Finally, I passed a sign with a Scottish flag and these words beneath it:

Welcome to Scotland

Fàilte gu Alba

A feeling of joy washed over me, it was as if I'd come home. I'd never set foot on Scottish soil but had felt called to this land for so long. I felt a smile spread across my face. I was here; at last. Tears filled my eyes at the realisation that I was experiencing positive feelings: excitement, anticipation, liberation, even joy.

Wasn't this how life should be? We get so caught up in our first world problems; stressing over the little stuff. Shouldn't we be going to the places that call to us? Enjoying the things that make us feel content?

I thought about my old job, my estranged husband back in my old home. My old life. How had I allowed myself to coast for so long?

And now here I was. Scotland. Why had I waited? I had no idea, but I was done putting things off. From now on, I was going to do what I felt called to do. No more procrastinating. I needed to enjoy this precious life.

I took a big deep breath and felt myself smile again.

It was as if the land had been whispering to me, calling me to visit my entire life. To walk in the footsteps of my grandparents, and my ancestors before them.

My paternal grandmother Nora grew up on a farm in Sutherland; my father, Frank, always said there wasn't anything she didn't know about grass, or sheep. She died before I was born, but I'd heard so much about her over the years. She was a happy, cheerful, kind woman who'd adored her family. Photos of her, although grainy, always showed a smiling face with hair just like mine, blonde and wavy with a bit of frizz. I always wished I'd had the chance to know her.

Her husband, my Grandad Tom, who gave me the precious journal currently sitting on my passenger seat, went on an adventure in 1960 with his friend Mike. They saved up all their money, set off in a Ford Anglia, and decided they'd travel around the whole of Britain for a year. A month into their trip, they'd arrived at my great-grandfather's farm, looking for some work for a few weeks to top up their funds.

Tom met Nora and they fell in love. It always sounded so romantic when Grandad told me the story; beautiful scenery, long walks holding hands, sneaking away from the farmhouse to steal a kiss in a nearby field.

I hadn't read the journal fully. Grandad Tom gave it to me and suggested I used it as a guide, follow his journey, read it as I go. Tempted though I was, I'd only flicked through to get a rough idea of my route. It was mostly black and white photos, maps, and some handwritten notes. Towards the back were some small sketches, and a different handwriting, from my grandmother, Nora. I'd always longed to know more about her and felt sad that she'd died so young. Tom was still alive, living in a retirement home, and doing well for his age.

Not long after crossing the border, I turned off to my first Scottish stop: Gretna Green. I followed a few tourist signs until I found the Blacksmiths Shop, which was the first place Grandad Tom had on his map. There was a large metal sculpture in the entrance to the carpark spelling out the word 'LOVE', loaded up with couple's padlocks. I wondered for a moment how many of the couples who got married here would end up like me, separated from the person they'd thought would be *the one*, and totally alone.

I shook my head. This was a romantic place. A place of hope. I wasn't going to let my own poor experience ruin this. I sat in my car and let myself relax for a moment. I'd left my sister's house early that morning feeling anxious, unsure about driving on my own, worried about taking the wrong turn. I hadn't spent much time alone before; I'd never lived by myself or travelled solo.

And yet here I was. I realised I hadn't had a panic attack for a while now. I felt calm and peaceful for the first time in ages.

I had very little idea what that future might look like, and I knew my savings would run out if I didn't get a job and settle as soon as my trip was over. But that was okay. The unlimited possibilities thrilled me.

'Thank you, Universe,' I whispered out loud in my car. I was determined that between the psychotherapy and this trip, it'd be the making of a new me. A me that sought adventure, that found a job she loved, a life she loved. I wasn't completely better, but there was hope now. Hope and excitement about what *could* be.

I picked up the journal and opened the first page. A fresh, crisp sheet of A5 had been paperclipped inside.

Dear Marianne,

As you've always wanted to visit Scotland, I am gifting you my journal.

I loved the beauty of the mountains, the clear waters of the lochs – and the sea! Spotting a fair few magnificent stags and, of course, drinking whisky whenever I could.

As you know, it was always a special place for me, especially meeting your grandmother, the love of my life!

If you're reading this, I hope you're planning or already on your own trip. I hope Scotland lives up to your expectations.

Be prepared to see every shade of green!

Enjoy, darling girl.

Lots of love,

Grandad Tom x

I felt my eyes fill with tears as I read it over again and ran my fingers lightly over the black ink. *Every shade of green...* perhaps the scenery could heal me, make me feel whole again.

I tucked the paper back into the clip and turned the first page. Grandad had written a little detail about Gretna and its history. In 18th-century England, couples had to be 21 before they could marry without their parents' consent. By contrast, you could marry in Scotland on the spot, with a simple ceremony. This led to many couples driving north and getting married just over the border.

Having read many regency romance novels, encouraged by my mother, I'd always associated Gretna as a place that caused scandal. In *Pride and Prejudice,* the thought that Elizabeth Bennett's sister Lydia could run off to Gretna with the villainous Mr Wickham was a major upset; the family would have never lived down the shame and would be ruined, forced to withdraw from polite society.

And yet Grandad described it as a place of romance. Where couples could unite forever, regardless of what their parents thought.

Time for me to check it out for myself. I wandered through the buildings, reading about the history and browsing the gift shops. A fizz of romance was in the air as a few newlyweds posed for photos.

My mind drifted to my own wedding day and how happy I'd been at the time. So optimistic and full of feelings for Ethan. How had we gone from that, to falling out of love? From committing to a lifetime together, to this? We hadn't spoken much since I'd moved out. Divorce now felt inevitable.

I couldn't decide whether to view our marriage as a mistake, a waste, or a learning experience... If I wanted to be positive, the latter. But how could my marriage be just a 'learning experience' when it was supposed to have been a life-long commitment to my soul mate? I realised no one really knew, as I looked at the couples at Gretna. You just had to take a chance.

It wasn't a chance I'd be willing to take again, but I still had high hopes for the rest of the human population.

I sighed, pushing the thoughts away, determined to be more mindful and focused on the present. If only it were easy to do that.

The last time I'd seen my youngest sister, Tess, she'd given me a beautiful piece of amethyst. It was purple with streaks of white threaded through it, smooth, round and about 3cm in diameter. She'd told me it was good for anxiety. So, I carried it with me, rolling it around in my hand. I had never taken any interest in crystals and had no idea if this was a little piece of magic, or just a placebo. Either way, it helped and that was all that mattered. Maybe it was the stone, maybe it was Scotland, maybe it was all the progress I'd made in therapy, but I felt grounded. And, having felt so low for so long, and so unsure about what I'd do next... it was a liberating feeling.

I was doing this, and I was fine.

I grabbed some dinner, a healthy salad. Although I'd stopped binge-eating long ago and lost a little weight, my body was still a good few stone heavier than before, and I wanted to take better care of myself. I checked into a hotel, and got into bed.

My dad had texted me earlier in the day, to check I'd arrived safe. I told him yes, grateful that he'd asked. Despite having a Scottish mother, my dad hadn't visited for several decades; he'd never taken us to see his mother's homeland and I often wondered why. For a moment, I longed for him to be with me, sharing in this, reading through the journal together.

I sighed. Enough wishing for anything other than what was.

I'm here, and I'm fine. And I'm going to have a wonderful time.

And then I slept my first night under the Scottish sky; content and calm and feeling like I'd somehow come home.

Chapter Three

Nora. 1960

My Mother always complained that I was too wild, too much like a lad than a lass, too dirty, outside too much. I didn't really care what she thought. I enjoyed feeling the grass beneath my bare feet. I loved to sit with the lambs in the spring, and I always let the autumn rain soak me through until I couldn't cope with the shivering any longer.

Being outdoors felt magical. I pictured the fae folk coming out at night and wandering through the grass at my feet. I liked to talk to the moon, and stare at the stars on a clear night. In summer, when it barely got dark in the Highlands, I'd sneak out of the house and watch the sunrise just after midnight. I collected leaves, twigs, moss and anything else I could forage within walking distance. Nature fascinated me, intrigued me, excited me.

As I grew older, I wasn't sure what was expected of me. I didn't even know what I wanted my future to hold.

My elder brother Malcolm would take over my parent's highland farm one day. But what about me? I supposed I would get married, have babies, and repeat the life my mother had. It seemed rather boring. A friend from school had gone to Glasgow to learn office work, but I couldn't stand the thought of living in a crowded place after growing up on the farm.

I loved the land, the air, and the views from the top of the hill on a beautiful sunny evening. I wasn't sure I'd ever be able to leave the Highlands.

Until I met Tom.

He arrived at the farm on a warm Friday morning in May 1960. My parents let out a few rooms to travellers for a little extra income. I was peering out of my bedroom and saw the Ford Anglia pull up. Out hopped two young men and one of them was so handsome, I caught my breath.

The lads, Tom and , were only supposed to stay for a weekend at first. But they offered to help on the farm for a few weeks in exchange for free board, and my father was more than happy, as Malcolm had sprained an ankle and wasn't much use.

It began with a few shy looks. I couldn't help but gaze at him and smile whenever we passed each other, or when he sat down at our family table for a meal on a Sunday teatime.

It was a grey and wet day, the first time we properly spoke. I'd been for a long walk, setting out before the rain came, but getting soaked through by the time I made my way back. This was the norm; I'd done it a thousand times. There was something invigorating and refreshing about letting Mother Nature batter you up on a hill.

My hair was hanging wet around my shoulders, my dress was stuck to my skin, and I could see a drop of water hanging off the end of my nose as I opened the gate and walked through the yard towards the farmhouse front door. The rain had just stopped, and a little sun was peeking through the clouds.

'Oh, you're soaked!' Tom said, grinning as he came out with a cup of tea. 'Here, you probably need this more than I do.' He offered me his mug.

'Thank you,' I said, taking it and grinning at him. 'I'll make you another. Are you working up in the top field today?'

I always seemed to know where he was.

'I am,' he said, grinning. 'But dry yourself off first, you'll catch cold!'

'You can't catch colds from being cold and damp,' I told him, sipping my tea. 'Or else I'd be sick non-stop. I often walk in the rain.'

'I suppose if you love to walk, then you have to deal with rain in these parts.'

I nodded. 'I do love to walk.'

'I noticed,' he said, winking at me and wandered off back towards the field whence I'd come.

He'd noticed me. The thought thrilled me, and I went inside with a big smile on my face and a warm, glowing, fluttering feeling in my chest.

I changed, dried my hair off a little with a towel and made him a fresh mug of tea. I found him mending a fence for my father. Feeling bold, I offered to help, and I could tell he was surprised, but he let me hand him tools and prop up posts as he worked.

We chatted about all sorts of topics; the great Scottish weather and the landscape, which he loved. He also loved whisky and working outdoors.

'I'm glad you're pleased with Scotland,' I said, watching him bite his lip as he hammered a nail.

'I am,' he said, glancing at me before continuing. 'I must admit I love your accent, too.'

'Ah thanks,' I said, blushing. 'I've heard before that not all English people can understand us.' I gave a little laugh.

'I confess,' he said, turning to look at me. 'I struggled with a few people. But it's not the Scottish accent I love. It's yours. You've a beautiful voice, Nora.'

He looked away. 'Sorry, that was a bit forward.'

'No,' I said, putting my hand on his arm. 'Not at all. Thank you. I like your voice too.'

He smiled at me, and we returned to talking about Scotland, and his great adventure. He talked about other places they wanted to see, and I knew he'd be on his way again before long. The thought made me sad.

There had been a few lads who'd shown an interest in me, but no one I really liked. There was something about Tom; a calm, steady energy that made me feel safe. The future no longer held a question mark – if I could be with him, it would all make sense somehow. I went from wanting some sort of unique existence to fancying a very normal one. Perhaps we'd find a house in a little village. Tom could run the local store, and I'd help now and then. We'd raise children. Get a cat or a dog. Go on days out to the coast.

A few weeks went by, with plenty of interesting conversation but nothing more. He was kind, and occasionally we'd flirt a little, but he never tried to kiss me. It was rather frustrating.

One day, I decided that if Tom left without anything happening between us, I'd regret it for the rest of my life. So, mustering all my courage, I cornered him in the barn, and to my delight, he kissed me right back.

After a while, Mike left, and Tom stayed. He was a hard worker, and my family loved him, but our blossoming romance was a secret. I often wondered later if it would've been half so exciting if everyone had known.

We would sneak off together for long walks. Tom offered to drive me into town when groceries were needed. It wasn't long before everyone picked up on the way we looked at each other. And it wasn't long after that, we realised we were very much in love.

He still wanted to see more of Scotland, and most of the places on his map I'd never seen myself. So, we went off on short trips, for a day at a time, taking a picnic with us and driving to a remote spot, where we'd walk, take a few photos on his camera, and kiss under a star-filled sky before heading home. It felt perfect, and I didn't want it to end.

'The thing is,' Tom told me one day, after six months of wonderful, dizzying romance. 'I have a job waiting for me back home. I'm to take on my father's shoe making business.'

And so, me, little Nora, who never thought I'd leave the Highlands, let alone for *England*, got engaged to and married Tom, who apparently had never thought about marriage at all.

Our honeymoon was spent touring the western coast, finishing with a few days in Glencoe. We paddled in the freezing sea. We had picnics on chilly white beaches. We saw lochs, deer, and mountains. We ate haggis in pubs. We made love every night.

I'd miss this place, my beautiful homeland. But Tom was worth it.

We returned to the farm, just for a few nights. My parents seemed pleased to have me off their hands, but still gave me a warm goodbye.

'Haste ye back!' said Malcolm, my lovely brother, tears in both of our eyes as we hugged each other tight. I was so sad to leave, but so in love with my new handsome husband and very excited about our future.

Chapter Four

Marianne

It's funny how we all get stuck in routines. Mine had been something like this:

Get up, get ready, have breakfast. Always porridge or avocado on toast. Always sitting at the breakfast bar in our terraced house, in the same town I'd grown up in; Market Harborough.

Ethan would give me a kiss on the cheek and leave for work.

I'd go into the office, or work from home. I was an underwriter for an insurance company. I liked some of the people I worked with. That's pretty much all I can say about it. Every day was almost exactly the same.

Lunch. Usually a salad, although I treated myself to a crusty baguette from the local bakery on a Friday. I munched on more biscuits than was good for me. I sometimes popped out and got a fancy coffee. I know, right: I was living it up.

Dinner. Usually a rotation of the same ten meals. Ethan was quite fussy, so we didn't vary our menu often. Although, guess what, Friday nights we had a takeaway. Usually, pizza with a side of garlic bread.

Evenings. Television. Maybe read a book. Cup of tea. Bed.

Weekends, I'd clean the house, maybe visit my parents, sometimes Nancy or my sisters and I would meet up for lunch.

And repeat.

And repeat some more.

I wanted to go places; to see more of Britain, as well as further afield. I wanted days out, and seaside trips and adventure. I wanted to do something meaningful, find a job I loved and feel like I was somehow doing what I was *meant* to do, whatever that was.

But I felt I didn't have enough time, didn't have enough money... truth was, I didn't make time. And we had money, we just saved it for a 'rainy day' that never came.

So, quitting my job, leaving my husband, driving, alone, over two hundred miles north to Gretna was fairly daring for me.

I woke up that first morning and felt disorientated. My old friend Anxiety was back, doing a little dance just between my ribs, warning me I was on scary ground. Sometimes, it's hard to keep the positive thoughts and mindfulness going.

One of the things my therapist Sandra had taught me was to consider what it was that was worrying me, so I took a deep breath.

Money. I'd worked it all out and I could afford to take a few months off, so long as I was careful and didn't stay in too many fancy hotels. Ethan insisted I didn't contribute to any bills or the mortgage until I got back, and we worked it all out, one way or the other. Deep breath. Money was okay, for now.

The future. Well, that was completely unknown. The thrill of it yesterday seemed ludicrous this morning. Where would I end up? I supposed I'd find a job... Here, in Scotland perhaps? I liked that idea. A fresh start. New surroundings, new work, new people. Deep breath. The future would work itself out.

What next? As I asked myself this question, I realised the little anxiety gremlin doing a dance in my chest had subsided. It was more of a prod than a crazy dance. Another deep breath.

I sat up, forced a smile and got myself in the shower, dressed and re-packed my things. I was overcoming this. I would not let this anxiety stop me for one more moment.

I ate my breakfast in the hotel restaurant in Gretna, looking at my route and checking the next few pages of the journal to make sure I went to the same places that Grandad had.

'Planning a road trip?'

I looked up to find a woman about my age. Masses of curly dark hair, bright green eyes, a tiny sparkly nose stud and a genuinely warm smile.

'Uh, yes,' I said, gesturing at the battered journal. 'My Grandad went on a road trip and I want to follow in his footsteps.'

'Awesome. Mind if I join you?' she said. 'I mean, for breakfast, obviously! Not your trip!' she laughed a hearty laugh, and I couldn't help but like her instantly. I pulled out a chair.

'No, of course, sit down, please.' There weren't many tables free, and it would be quite nice to have company. My main concern about the trip – you know apart from my car breaking down in the middle of nowhere, being murdered and left to rot in a Scottish bog, etc. – was that I'd be lonely.

'I'm Luna,' she said, offering her hand which I shook.

'Marianne,' I told her, closing the journal.

'What a beautiful name!'

'I'm named after Marianne Dashwood, a Jane Austen character.'

'Oh, that's lovely. I've read *Sense and Sensibility*, watched the movie too, so you're named after Kate Winslet's character?'

'Yep,' I said. I'd had this conversation many times before. 'My sisters are Tess, from Thomas Hardy's novel, and Jane, after *Jane Eyre*. My mum loves historical romance.'

'Oh, I just love that.'

'And Luna, also a lovely name. Where did that come from?'

'Well, I confess my given name was Tammy. I love the moon, so I changed it.'

'Luna's a beautiful name, and it suits you.'

She gave me another warm smile and put her hand over mine. I'd usually dislike physical contact from a total stranger, but something about her touch was soothing, and a wave of calm energy washed over me.

'You've gone through a tough time, haven't you?'

I almost froze, the feeling gone. I only just resisted moving my hand out from under hers.

'Sorry,' she said, moving her hand away quickly. 'I shouldn't do that, we only just met.'

The server arrived with my breakfast and took Luna's order. Even when she was talking to him, she had warmth and an upbeat, enthusiastic charm.

'It's fine,' I told her once she was done. 'I was just a bit taken aback.'

'I have a habit of doing that,' she said, smiling.

'But you're right,' I admitted, feeling very open with her despite the surprise from her words, 'I have had a bit of a tough time. I've recently left my husband and quit my job.'

Luna reached out and put her hand back on mine.

'I'm sorry. You know what though, things are going to improve.'

'Oh really?' I couldn't help but grin. 'Are you psychic?'

'Yep,' she said without missing a beat. 'I have the gift of sight, and I'm very intuitive.'

'Wow, that's so interesting. Do you do readings for people?'

I immediately regretted asking. I had a budget to stick to and now I'd feel obliged to give this woman money to tell me something generic and obvious, given what she already knew. Something like *"you're going to go on your travels and meet a new man."*

But it didn't happen.

'Sometimes. I run a shop, up in Inverness. I sell crystals, esoteric supplies, that sort of thing. I offer reiki healing and workshops and run a local spiritual group.'

'That's amazing, I've always been curious about this sort of thing, my sister Tess is very spiritual. She gave me a piece of amethyst,' I took it out of my pocket and showed her.

She took the amethyst and gently held it in her hand.

'That's very kind of her.' She held it for a moment longer, then passed it back. 'That's a lovely piece. There's a full moon in a few days, leave it out on the windowsill that night, and it'll charge.'

I had no idea what this meant, how could you 'charge' a mineral item? I just smiled, somehow knowing I'd follow this advice, even though it felt a little weird.

'So, what brings you here?' she asked, and I told her about my trip. I pushed the journal towards her. 'Feel free to have a look, there's a map in the front although it's pretty old.'

She wiped her hands on her napkin, and carefully flipped through the journal.

'Sounds like a beautiful trip. It looks like he did a large section of what is now known as the NC500 route,' she told me, pointing to the map my grandad had drawn with coloured pencils. 'So that'll be easy, you can follow the tourist signs when you get up that way.'

'Very useful, thank you. So, what are you doing here in Gretna?'

'I've been down south visiting family,' Luna said, pulling a face and sighing.

'Not a happy visit?'

'My family don't really get me. They don't understand my business. And they don't like that I moved so far away. You'll understand why, though, when you see how wonderful it is.'

It was easy, being in Luna's company. Comfortable and comforting, too. She told me about her husband, her kids, her shop, her hobbies, and her beliefs in everything from crystals to witchcraft and spirits living among us. None of it felt strange, just fascinating. I realised that Luna was eccentric, magical, kind, open and honest. I loved her.

She asked me about my life, my family, my marriage, and my work. I wasn't used to opening up to strangers, but I felt like I'd known her forever as I shared my story. I had intended to get on the road early, but lunchtime came, and I found myself ordering more food.

'Pass me your phone,' Luna told me as we stood at our cars saying goodbye. I handed it to her. 'Here's my number,' she said as she tapped it in. 'Text or call whenever you want to. And when you get over my way, come and visit me.'

'Oh, that'd be lovely,' I told her, surprising myself. I had made a friend. I had someone to go and visit, and that felt nice... more than nice. It felt *right*.

'I cannot wait to see you and hear about what you've seen and done between now and then! And take this,' she pushed a small, smooth crystal into my hand. It was a deep green colour with darker green stripes, and it was beautiful. 'It's malachite. Good for travels.'

'That's so lovely, thank you,' I said, overcome by how much I liked her in just a short space of time. 'I definitely will come and visit you.'

'Good. Now go enjoy yourself, have an amazing trip.'

She gave me a quick but tight hug. I watched her drive away, and something deep down inside my being told me that I'd just made a friend for life.

I was in Edinburgh by late-afternoon. I checked into my hotel and went out to Princes Street. Overwhelm flooded me as both locals and tourists alike buzzed past me, on a mission to shop, or sight-see, or find food. I was surrounded by people but somehow had never felt more alone. I almost turned back to my car, ready to head further north, to retreat into the hills and mountains I'd been dreaming about. Then I looked up at the castle and decided I had to see this through.

I took a big deep breath, told myself not to panic and held my two crystals. I had no idea if they would help, but I felt grounded and stronger just by circling them in my hands as I walked. Maybe there was something in it, after all.

Rain started to trickle as I climbed the cobbled steep slopes up to the castle. I didn't mind getting a little wet and couldn't help but wonder what Ethan would have said, he would have complained no doubt. About the weather, about arriving later than planned...

Suddenly, I felt empowered. No one complaining. Or dictating what I do. No compromises to be made. This trip was all about me, and whatever I wanted to do.

I roamed the castle, skim-read the information boards, and looked out at the view of Edinburgh. It felt familiar. Like I'd been here before, even though I knew I hadn't. I wondered if I was picking up on some sort of ancestral memory, if such a thing was possible. Had Nora been here? Had any of my ancestors lived here, worked here, fought at the castle?

I ate the most amazing vegetarian haggis with neeps and tatties (potatoes and swede) in a pub near the hotel and sipped a big glass of red wine while I read about Grandad's time here. He and his friend had walked all over the city and visited the castle. In the evening, they got drunk with some locals they'd met randomly in an unnamed pub.

I tried to picture him, a young man, free and single, his whole life ahead of him. With no idea that he'd meet the love of his life in only a matter of weeks.

I had a small glass of whisky and held up a silent toast to him and his friends, for leading me on this adventure. Once again, I enjoyed a peaceful, relaxing sleep.

Chapter Five

Marianne

Next stop: Stirling. Or so I thought.

As I drove along the motorway, I spotted something kind of beautiful: two horse sculptures standing thirty metres high. I detoured immediately. The Kelpies: I'd heard of them, seen photos, but had no idea I'd be passing them so closely.

There was hardly anyone else around as I set off on foot from the car park to get a better view. The closer I got, the more fascinated I was. It was sunny, with just a few clouds and I felt the vitamin D soaking into my pores; I hadn't expected much good weather, but the forecast was looking good.

I passed a visitor centre, but my eyes were mesmerised by the magnificent horse heads emerging from the ground. Eventually, I was right beneath, and I stared up at the shiny steel for a little while, watching birds flit inside the hollow structures, and out again.

I took a few photos, then walked away to admire them better. I found a bench, and sat down for a while, watching different people arriving to get a closer look; photographers, couples, families with children running about, walkers and their dogs.

There was something about this man-made wonder, something so beautiful. I felt overcome with emotion for a moment, so glad I'd made this trip. But then I looked around and realised I had no one to share it with. After years of being in a relationship, a *marriage*, I became acutely aware of how silent my day had been.

I needed to speak to someone.

I got out my phone and called Nancy, but she didn't answer. I had no idea why, but next I tried Luna. Despite our one-time meeting, I felt like we'd bonded, and I needed a friend.

'Marianne! Where are you? Around Edinburgh? Or Stirling?'

'Between the two, I'm at the Kelpies.'

'Oh, lovely. I've never been up close, but from the motorway, they're just wonderful.'

'They are,' I said, swallowing a lump in my throat. I realised I'd called her to tell her I wouldn't make it to Inverness. The thought of continuing felt too lonely.

'I hope this isn't to say that you're not going to make it up to Inverness,' Luna said, picking up on the emotion in my voice.

Of course, she knew.

I could hear her doing something in the background and imagined her sorting through the stock in her shop, surrounded by crystals and incense, dreamcatchers and windchimes. For a microsecond, I wanted to say I'd still come; just to see it for myself. Then reality caught up with me.

'I'm sorry, I'm just not sure I can do this on my own, I was silly to think I could. I'm feeling lonely today and this sort of trip just isn't for me. But thank you for the wonderful offer to stay. Maybe I'll take you up on it another time.'

'Do you want sympathy or tough love?'

'I guess, sympathy?'

'Well, you're getting both!'

I couldn't help but smile.

'Okay, give it to me.'

'What makes you think you can't do this?'

'I'm too emotional for one. And I'm thirty-five! Hardly the age to go off adventuring alone. Most of my friends back home are married and settled with kids.'

'Marianne, take a breath.'

I did as she said.

'Do you want to be married and settled with children?'

'Ethan, my husband, does,' I told her. 'We've recently separated. I always wanted pets to be honest, not kids. I don't know why, and no one else seemed to get it, but I just never felt that maternal urge, you know?'

'I do know, I've got a friend who feels the same way. And that's fine, having kids is bloody hard work, and there is nothing wrong with not wanting to do it. It's not for everyone.'

'I know it's fine, I guess it's everyone else's expectations. My parents, Ethan, even friends. They ask me all the time and drop hints. It makes me feel like I'm being selfish, or that there's something wrong with me.'

Poor Luna, I was treating her like a therapist, and we'd only just met. I was determined to make our future friendship more about her, less about me.

'There's nothing wrong with you, Marianne! There are many paths, many types of life to choose. Parenthood may not be for you. Please stop punishing yourself for not being who others want you to be!'

Of course, she was right. I sat up a little straighter. She could be a motivational speaker.

'You're right.' Of course, she was right. Sometimes you know what's true, but you need to hear it from someone else before you really believe it.

'An adventure like this is a chance to find yourself, to connect with the most authentic, real you. To figure out what you want in life. So, what's *really* stopping you?'

I sat up a little straighter as I thought about this crucial question. 'Fear. Loneliness.'

'I thought as much,' she said, and I could hear her fiddling around in the background again, doing who knew what. I suddenly wanted to be there, to browse her magical store and buy her a glass of wine and talk about her life, and mine.

'Fear is just an acronym for False Evidence Appearing Real. So, kick that one right away.'

I laughed. 'Okay.'

'And of course, you're lonely because you've never done anything like this before. But I reckon you'll adapt and get used to it. And I'm here if you ever want to talk. I'm sure you've got other friends too. Get in touch with people. But also learn to enjoy your own company. Because from what I've seen you're an awesome person to be around.'

I laughed again.

'You're very kind, you only met me for a few hours.'

'I know, and this sounds crazy, but I feel like we bonded more in those few hours than I do with some friends over years of knowing them. I can't wait to see you when you visit me, which you will, because you're not turning back.'

'Me too,' I said, finally relaxing. 'I'm going to continue. Thank you, Luna. You don't know how much I needed this conversation.' I found my two crystals, and let their mystical powers wash over me as I rolled them around in my palm.

'Okay so you're good? Don't turn back now or you'll totally regret it for the rest of your days. You owe it to yourself. To your Grandad! To the universe!' she said on a high.

'I do,' I said, nodding and smiling as I looked at the Kelpies again. 'Thank you.'

'Would you rather be at your desk, doing your boring old job, or there, staring up at the Kelpies?'

'Here, of course,' I admitted. *Of course.*

'Well think of all the other memories and experiences you're about to create. You've been gifted this time, this place, this life. Go enjoy it. Push your comfort zone. I won't hear another word about turning back. Go get a coffee, some lunch, whatever. Pull yourself together woman. Get back in that car and get to Stirling.'

'Okay, okay, I'm convinced.' And I really was.

'Good. That's all my motivational ideas used up.'

I laughed. 'Oh, Luna. I just…' I was laughing and teary, now '…thank you.'

'Don't thank me. Just do it. And I know someday I'll call you in a flap and you'll need to talk me down.'

'Anytime.'

We said our goodbyes and I stared at my phone for a moment. What had I done to deserve a friend like this? I glanced back up at the Kelpies, thanked the universe, then stood and stretched. On I would go. I went to the bathroom and stared at my puffy red eyes.

Hadn't I shed enough tears this past year? And I didn't even know why. Nothing terrible had happened to me, people fell out of love all the time. I hadn't been dumped. No one had died. I had money in the bank and free time to travel for a bit. I was incredibly fortunate. I'd just lost my way a bit. I needed to find myself again, and I wasn't going to do that back home.

I'd come this far, in the hope of Scotland somehow healing me, and in a very small way, it already had. I couldn't give up. I needed to work out what the next chapter of my life would be.

I had a feeling the new Marianne was going to be unlike all previous versions. I hoped for a stronger, more resilient, happier, more content version. One who knew which job would fulfil her. What sort of relationship she wanted, if at all.

I suddenly felt very self-aware, thinking of the decisions I'd made in the past. Ethan was handsome, kind and very interested in me. And that is why we got together. I'd loved him because he loved me. But we didn't share the same values, goals, or ambitions.

Breaking up had been the hardest decision I'd ever made in my life and separating our lives had been incredibly painful. If I were ever to meet anyone again, surely it had to be someone I could build a life together with, a future that made us both happy? Instead of compromising and holding each other back?

I took a deep breath. I felt like I'd had an epiphany. It wasn't that I wasn't willing to fall in love again. It was that I wasn't willing to fall in love with the wrong person again. This buoyed me, and I pictured a perfect match, a faceless man, out there waiting to meet me. I just hadn't met him yet, and nor was I ready to... but, somehow, this made me feel less lonely.

I stared at my reflection for a few minutes. *You got this*; she told me. *Let's do it.*

As I got back in my car, I saw that Luna had texted me:

See you when you reach Inverness!

I still hesitated as I set up the map. It would still be easier to head back south, back to England. Perhaps even back to Ethan. Back to the desk job.

Then I thought about standing on a Scottish hill, looking down into the valley below. Perhaps there'd be a loch. Perhaps I'd see a stag like Grandad had.

Going home might *feel* easy right now, but I'd soon be depressed again.

I smiled to myself. I was going to do this. No more doubts. I was where I was meant to be if I could only get out of my own way. I got back out of my car, marched back to the visitor centre, and bought a nice pen and a beautiful notebook with the Kelpies embossed on the front. One last quick glance at the horses, then I marched back, sat in my car, and tore the cellophane off the notebook. I wrote a little about my day, the epiphany I'd had, my feelings and my hopes for the future. I felt like the new me was finally emerging.

I started the car, got on the motorway, and was on my way to Stirling.

Chapter Six

Nora. 1962

Tom and I set up home in a two-bedroom mid-terrace house in Northampton, partially funded by his parents. Of course, it was very different from my former life on a Highland farm. For the first few months, I missed it all madly; my family and friends, the open spaces and scenery, the trees, wildlife, and the sheep. Everything felt different, from the accents to the smells, to the way of life.

Tom worked hard with his father, but he was always home in time for tea. My mother had taught me how to cook and I delighted in providing a clean home and putting food on the table.

Who knew what his parents thought when he returned from Scotland with a bride, but they were welcoming, and his mother Esther and I got on very well. Sometimes, Tom would go with his father, Michael, to watch the local football team, while Esther and I would go for a wander around the market or bake cakes together. Esther's father had been a baker and she taught me how to make bread, cakes, scones, and tarts. I also got a job working at a haberdashery shop and made a few friends.

Once I settled in, those first few years were happy ones. Tom was kind and attentive. We saw my family a few times a year, despite the long drive.

After a few years Frank came into our world. I wasn't one of those women who bonds with their baby from the moment they realise they're carrying, and I must admit I didn't enjoy the first few months of being a mother. Tom was working and my own mother was too far away to help. I felt too proud to admit to Esther that I was struggling. Tom would set off for work, and Frank and I would sit together all day. He slept a lot, and I cried a lot.

Esther realised my struggle though, and being the kind of woman she was, she came and helped me. She showed me how to bathe the baby, the best way to get nappies clean and encouraged me to sleep while she cleaned my house. Things got better after that.

Tom's father retired, and he took over the business, which meant we could move into a larger house. By 1965 we had another baby, a beautiful girl whom we called Moira.

This time, somehow, I thrived - even though I had two wee bairns to manage at once. Frank was almost three when Moira was born so he tried to help a little, bringing toys to shake in front of her and passing me her blanket when she was cold.

I asked my family to come visit, but they said they couldn't leave the farm. I suggested just Mam came, with Malcolm perhaps, on the train. But no. It couldn't be done. It was too far to take two young children, so we didn't see each other for a few years. My mother wasn't a fan of the telephone, so we wrote letters.

Although I missed them; I loved my life, I loved my little family. Most of all, I loved my Tom.

On the last weekend of every month, Esther and Michael would come to our house and stay with the children while Tom and I went out, just the two of us. Sometimes we'd have a quiet meal, or a picnic if the weather was nice. We'd go for a walk or take a drive out to the countryside so I could enjoy some open space. I missed the views from back home.

I often found myself thinking of the future. What would Frank and Moira grow up to do? When would they marry and have children? Where would they live and how often would I see them? I'd create little fantasies of our futures in my head; perhaps Frank would be a builder or carpenter as he loved playing with building blocks. Moira liked to sing, and I imagined her being famous, on the world stage.

It was our sixth wedding anniversary, and Tom took me out to a lake for a picnic supper. He had asked his mother to pack up the food in a hamper. We had fresh bread, cheese, salad, homemade lemonade, and a beautiful fruit cake, wrapped up in wax paper.

'It's good to be outdoors,' I told him. 'It's nice to be surrounded by scenery.'

'You gave up a lot for me,' Tom said, nibbling on some cheese. 'I hope I am living up to it.'

'Oh sweetheart,' I put my hand on his. 'I love our life, but I'm not sure living in a town is for me long term.'

We started discussing where else we might live. Tom suggested we move out to a more rural location. The children would have more space to roam as they grew older. We could keep chickens, perhaps. Get a dog. It sounded idyllic.

By the time we were eating the fruit cake, we were already discussing locations and the type of house we might afford. Tom suggested I learn to drive, which hadn't even occurred to me before now.

So, we moved out of Northampton, to a quiet village on the border with Leicestershire. It wasn't too far for Tom to drive to work. I met new friends. We built a life; a simple but happy one.

Chapter Seven

Marianne

Luna had recommended a hotel with a nice restaurant in Stirling, so I headed there, and checked in. I had a lovely chat with the very friendly owner, found myself a seat in the restaurant by a window, and sipped a lovely glass of wine whilst taking in the décor. To think I could have been sitting on the M6, heading south by now... I smiled to myself. I was here, in Scotland, and I was doing this. I decided I wouldn't doubt myself again.

This place was lovely, a whole wall full of artificial flowers in pinks and whites. Fairy lights strung all over, and oak tables with comfortable seats. Outside the window I could people-watch as folks went about their business.

Nancy called me back, and as I stared at her name on my phone, I wondered what advice she'd have given me if she'd answered when I was at the Kelpies. Would I still be here now, or heading home?

'Hi Nancy.'

'So sorry I missed your call!' she said without a greeting. 'You okay? How's it going? Tell me everything.'

So, I did, I gave her a summary of Gretna, and Edinburgh, and the Kelpies. She listened, chipping in words about how lovely it all sounded and how envious she was. I didn't mention my wobble because it was over, and I wanted to keep it positive.

'How're you?'

'I'm good, you know, the usual, the kids are all-consuming. I saw Ethan today in Waitrose.'

I realised with a smile that I didn't care that much.

'Did you speak to him?' I asked, turning my wine glass around absentmindedly, not sure I wanted to know what he had to say.

'Yeah, it was a bit awkward, we just made small talk. He looked tired.'

She went on to tell me about her kids, and a recent shopping trip to buy new lounge furniture... and I made all the right noises while I listened; but I couldn't help feeling slightly detached. I didn't have a lounge anymore. I didn't care much for material possessions. Nancy and I had been close, up until a few years ago, but as she chatted, I noticed just how little we had in common. Our lives were very different since she'd had children, and I knew I wouldn't tell her about the crystals, or the strong connection I felt to Scotland. I wouldn't even tell her about how I was feeling closer, somehow, to my grandmother, Nora, who I'd never even met. We just didn't have that sort of friendship anymore, we'd grown apart.

Our conversations, I realised, were superficial. We floated around on trivial topics these days. We'd drifted apart, and while that was sad, I wondered if that was all part of this new evolution of myself, finding new people as well as new places.

As we ended the call, I pulled out my new journal and wrote...

One of my intentions for this trip is to figure out who I am, and what I want. That isn't just about where I live and what I do for a living. It's about the people I surround myself with. Ethan, Nancy and even my family are all nice people, but are they MY people? I want to connect with like-minded souls, who talk about deep and meaningful stuff. Who have a sense of adventure and a wonderful spiritual spark about them. I want to feel grounded, confident and ALIVE. I set this intention, for the universe to help me. Allow me to be the most authentic version of myself. To meet others who will support and love me for who I am. Send me joy, adventure and make me self-aware.

I re-read it a few times. I'd never done anything like this before, talking to the universe, setting intentions, delving deep into what I truly wanted from my life. I thought of Luna, one of the few people I knew who'd probably get it. I sent her a quick text to let her know I'd arrived in Stirling and to thank her for the hotel/restaurant recommendation. I ordered a veggie ravioli dish and, for once, I enjoyed my own company.

I went to bed early, enveloped in a heavy duvet with pale tartan covers. I read some more of Grandad Tom's journal, and looked up what to do the following day.

I thought of Grandad back in his retirement home near Market Harborough, pictured him tucked up asleep in his bed. Did he dream of Nora, I wondered? He'd gone nearly half his life as a widower, never remarrying. I hugged the journal to my chest.

'Thanks Grandad.' I whispered, just before I fell asleep.

Stirling Castle is on a hill, easily walkable from the centre of town, and the views there are spectacular. I let the wind whip my hair and literally felt it sweep the cobwebs out of my old life as my new one was taking form.

'It's windy, isn't it!' a young girl said to me, grinning as her hair swept around her face crazily, same as mine.

'Yes, but beautiful!' I said, grinning back before returning my eyes to the view. I could see the National Wallace Monument, a huge tower, standing tall and proud on a hill in the distance. Despite the wind, it was a sunny day, clouds moving across the sky, and casting shadows on the landscape below. I took a deep breath, allowing the crisp air to fill my lungs, picturing my new start, my new life, whipping me up in the air. I wanted to shout 'freeeedom!' Mel Gibson style, with my hands in the air, but there were too many people around. That's what I'd found, I realised, *freedom*. And it felt wonderful.

'It's still very windy, isn't it!' said the girl, who had run off but appeared again. I smiled at her. She was about five, I'd guess. She had glorious red wavy hair, which was being swept about by the wind and she tucked it behind her ears, only for it to flail about again.

'Indeed, it is,' I said, grinning. 'My hair is going crazy.'

'Mine too!' she giggled. 'Where are you from?'

'I'm from a small town called Market Harborough, in Leicestershire,' I told her. 'How about you?'

'I'm from Scotland,' she said, attempting to tie her hair back in a blue scrunchie. 'Can you tell from my accent?'

'I can.' I glanced around, looking for an adult but I couldn't see anyone nearby.

'I live near Aviemore,' she told me, coming to stand beside me and leaning on the castle wall. Aviemore was on my list to visit later in the trip, but I couldn't remember the exact location.

'How did you get all the way here,' I asked, 'I hope the wind didn't blow you?'

She giggled. 'No, my dad drove us. I'm visiting my Nana and Grandpops.'

'Where are they now?' I asked, glancing around again for her adults.

'Somewhere round here with my dad.'

'Do they know where you are?'

She gave me another grin. 'I thought it'd be fun to look around on my own.'

'Don't you think they'll be worried about you?'

She shrugged. 'Maybe.'

'Shall I help you find them?' I asked, then I saw a man walking towards us.

'Iona,' he called, and she spun round. 'Iona, I've been looking all over for you!'

She shouted sorry but stayed still. 'I've made a new English friend!' she told him.

I smiled, and he gave me a relieved smile back. Handsome. Light brown hair. Broad shoulders, wearing a dark blue fleece, cargo trousers and walking boots. An outdoorsy type, I decided.

'I hope you're not bothering this lady,' he said kindly. He held out a hand to her, 'come on, we'd better find Nana and Pops, they'll be worried.'

His eyes lingered on mine for a few moments as she walked towards him, which set little sparks of pleasure zapping around my entire being. It'd been a long time since I'd really looked at other men, and I caught my breath for a moment, realising I found him attractive. After so many years of being with the same person, and so many months trying to get over the fact he wasn't my happily ever after, it felt good to sense a little chemistry.

'Bye!' said Iona, waving as she took his hand, and he led her off.

'Enjoy the rest of your day!' I called after them.

I wandered around a little longer until my stomach started to rumble. I found my way to the café and took out my journal again. I felt the need to write about Ethan.

We met on a sunny January day in my hometown of Market Harborough. I was 25 years old, just about ready to meet someone I could be serious about. I was working at a small insurance firm, and he came in to have a meeting with the owner. Ethan invested in other businesses and made a lot of money from it. Even ten years later, I didn't fully understand what he did or why he was so good at it.

Our first few dates went so well, I was sure he was the one for me. He seemed so kind, so romantic, so interested in me. He sent flowers, bought me a beautiful bracelet, and took me to fancy restaurants. He felt grown up and, between his financial stability and sensible attitude towards life, offered me a lot of security.

I realised I was in love with him that Easter; we went to the Cotswolds for a long weekend, and I suddenly couldn't see a future without him.

We were together a year before I moved in, and shortly after that he proposed. I was so sure he was the one. That we'd be together forever.

Our wedding was a medium-size affair, about 100 guests. Nice hotel. Stunning white dress that I'd since donated to charity. Nancy and my sisters were bridesmaids. Mum and Dad, to my relief, managed to make pleasant conversation despite rarely seeing each other since their divorce. Grandad Tom even shed a few tears, telling me how wonderful it was to see me in love and happy.

So, I asked myself as I wrote about this in my journal, what had happened? Where did that love go? Had we drifted apart, perhaps? And if so, that was fine, more than fine. It was natural, normal, and meant to be.

However, I realised, looking back, that love we'd had was not built on a good foundation. It was an attraction to a kind and decent person who I met at the right time when I was ready to settle down. But we didn't talk about what a good life looked like, we just got swept along in the romance of it all without stopping to consider if we were even a good fit for the long haul. You can't grow old with someone who doesn't want the same things as you. This trip was a perfect example; we didn't even like the same holidays. Come to think of it, we didn't have much in common at all.

Relationships took work, and I wanted a simple life. But to write-off men forever didn't feel right either...

Flings. I smiled. Not my usual style, but maybe flings would be my future? Have fun, enjoy a little lust and romance, then move on before things got messy. Better than being single, but better than risking another broken heart.

'Hi again!' Iona ran over, interrupting my reflection time.

'Oh hello,' I said, glancing up to see her dad and grandparents taking a seat nearby. Talking of lust, he was very nice to look at.

'I'm Iona,' she said, holding out her hand. I shook it. She was wearing a cute top with a highland cow on it.

'I'm Marianne. It's very nice to meet you again. I love your top.'

'Thank you. My dad said I'm not to bother you for more than two minutes.'

'Oh really,' I glanced over at him. He was in conversation with a man I assumed was his father, they looked alike. 'Well, I don't mind at all,' I told Iona. 'Truth is, you're the most conversation I've had all day.'

'Don't you have any family or a boyfriend, or a husband?'

'Well,' I loved this kid's boldness so I decided to be honest. 'I am technically married but right now I'm travelling on my own.'

'Where's your husband then?'

'Well, we broke up.'

She sighed dramatically, bless her. 'That must make you sad.'

'It did, but it's easier now.'

'I'm just going for a wee,' she said suddenly, running off. I looked back down at my journal and closed it.

'I'm sorry about Iona.' Her dad appeared. 'She craves female company; she lost her mother.'

'Oh gosh I'm so sorry,' I said, my heart breaking for her.

'Thanks. She was just a baby when it happened, but I find her talking to random women all the time.'

'Bless her.'

'Thank you for being kind to her.'

'Not at all.'

I glanced over his shoulder. 'She's coming back.'

'Daddy! I told you she's nice. Her name is Marianne. Isn't she pretty?'

I felt myself immediately blush. 'Very,' he said, smiling at me again. 'Now, come along.'

'Nice to meet you Iona,' I said again. 'And you,' I said, smiling at her dad.

'My name is Finn,' he said, smiling. 'Goodbye, Marianne.'

There was something about his eyes; they were hazel, a swirl of green and brown. Beautiful. Easy to gaze into.

'Have fun at the castle!' Iona said as she pulled Finn by the hand towards her grandparents.

'Don't let the wind blow you over!' I called back.

Iona giggled as they drifted away, leaving me in a flustered tizz at the thought of her handsome dad.

Back at my hotel, I looked at myself in the mirror. After all that binge-eating and lack of activity, I had become fairly overweight, and had to buy clothes two sizes bigger than a few years ago. I turned to the side, remembering the tingly fizzy feeling I'd felt seeing Finn earlier. There was no way a man like him could be interested in a woman like me. Overweight, lacking in confidence, no job, no home, not to mention that he'd seen me with crazy wild hair. He was just being nice, and I got carried away, thinking there was a spark.

It'd been nice to believe, for a moment, though.

Chapter Eight

Marianne

The next five days flew by, buoyed by the idea I might feel attracted to someone other than Ethan, and the fact I'd got this far. Plus, encouraging texts from Luna and uncharacteristic non-stop Scottish sunshine helped... I enjoyed my time in Stirling, enjoyed driving to Perth, and then Aberdeen. The further North I went, the more at ease I felt. I'd never been to these places, and yet they felt familiar, like I was home.

I walked quaint streets, then barefoot on cool beaches. I chatted to locals and tourists, and I slept soundly, every night.

'Marianne?'

'Hi, Grandad.'

'Where are you?'

'I'm not far from Aberdeen. I'm driving into the Cairngorms later today.'

'Ah, wonderful. One of my favourite places on Earth. You'll love it, my dear. And have you been drinking whisky?'

'Every chance I get,' I told a white lie. I'd had a few but preferred a red wine. 'Grandad, it's been wonderful.'

'So how long will you be in the Cairngorms?'

'A week, you said it was worth a reasonable stay?'

'It is. Get some of that fresh air in your lungs. Can you send a text to your Aunt Moira with the address you're staying at? She has something for you.'

Aunt Moira was Dad's sister, I'd not seen her in ages. 'Yes of course. That's nice.'

We chatted for a while longer, Grandad clearly thrilled I was tracing his footsteps and then telling me all the news from home. My sisters had been to visit him, and Dad too. He told me to check the journal for the places he'd visited, and described the views with such enthusiasm I almost hung up, just to get on with it, to get to this place he loved.

The drive into the Cairngorms was all he'd said and more, in fact his words had barely done it justice. At every corner was a different stunning vista. I passed pine trees and glorious purple heather. I saw birds of prey, and even deer. I kept stopping to take photos and posted a few online when I had a signal.

I ate my lunch on a small patch of grass, allowing my bare feet to touch the earth, feeling totally and completely at one with the land.

'Thank you, Scotland,' I whispered as I got back into the car.

Home for the next seven nights was a small cottage in a village called Carrbridge. It was nice to finally unpack a few things, and it gave me a chance to do some laundry. Starving hungry, I looked up the nearest supermarket so I could get some supplies.

Aviemore. 15 minutes' drive away. I thought of Iona and wondered if they'd returned from Stirling yet.

Aviemore is a nice little town, with a raft of tourist and outdoor stores. So, after filling my car with snacks, frozen pizzas, and other necessities, I had a wander around the shops, and bought myself some new hiking boots and a waterproof coat. The weather looked set to turn in a few days and I wanted to get outside as much as possible before then. Grandad had climbed a particular hill and mentioned it in the journal, so I was determined to do the same one, albeit a little nervous on the idea of going by myself.

I was just getting back to my car when I heard a male voice.

'Marianne!'

I silently thanked the universe as I turned and saw Finn, revelling in the serendipity of the moment. Turning to greet my new friends, I noticed Iona wasn't with him.

'Oh, Finn, hi!' I said, taken aback once again by his charming smile and feeling my insides zing at how attractive I found him.

'Going hiking?' he said, gesturing to my shopping bags.

'Planning to, I'm here for a week. How's Iona?'

'Oh, she's staying down in Stirling with my parents for a fair while,' he said as I got lost in those gorgeous hazel eyes again. I had to lean back on my car a little to steady myself. It'd been so long since I'd felt this way, I wasn't sure how to handle it.

'Ah that's nice.'

'Yes, they take her for school holidays.'

'I see.'

'Do you want to...' he looked away, and I was surprised to see him blush. I was making a man blush! 'Sorry, you've probably got plans...'

'No, I mean, I do want to... whatever you were going to suggest...' I stammered, like some young girl who couldn't compose herself. He might be about to suggest I help him clean his house and I was just agreeing. I told myself to get a grip and stood a little taller.

'Umm. Sorry, I just remembered that Iona said you were married.'

'Ah. Well, technically, I am. Separated.'

I saw a flicker of something in his eyes. But seriously, he was way out of my league.

'Would you like to get something to eat? There's a pub just down the road, you could follow me there. They make a great veggie curry.'

'How did you...'

'In Stirling, at the café,' he said softly. 'You asked the staff if the sandwich was vegetarian.'

'Well remembered,' I said, sure my face was as pink as his.

'So, I'll follow you?'

He grinned. 'Yep. I'm in the grey VW over there.'

The pub was called The Dragon, and it was one of those places that's warm and welcoming from the moment you walk in. It smelt of whisky and good food and the woman behind the bar welcomed us as we arrived. We found a table by the window, and I could hardly believe this man, this handsome, fit, gorgeous man would want to take me for something to eat.

'So, are you travelling all over?' Finn asked as he took a sip of his pint. A glass of pinot noir, for me.

I told him about Grandad Tom and showed him the journal.

'This is amazing,' he said, carefully turning each page, reading some of the anecdotes and holding up the photos to get a closer look.

'From here I'm going to travel the NC500 route with a few detours, looks like I'll cover a lot of the journey my grandad did?'

'Yes, for sure. This is going to sound contrived, but that's what I'm planning to do while Iona is away.'

My head swirled. He was going on a similar trip. So, we could have multiple evenings like this one. If I wanted to. If he wanted to. If we wanted to.

Did I want to be *we* again, yet?

I silently told myself to stop getting carried away and respond in a normal fashion.

'Blimey, amazing coincidence!' I managed to say, hoping I didn't look alarmed. I was alarmed at the thought of 'we' but not at the thought of spending more time with him.

'Don't worry, I'm not going to stalk you,' he said, winking and picking up the menu. 'I don't know why I'm looking; I always pick the vegetable curry.'

'Then I will too,' I said, pushing it away. 'So, tell me all about Iona.'

His face broke into a grin. 'She's awesome. Really intelligent. Amazing artist, brilliant for her age. Loves the outdoors. She keeps me on my toes.'

'I bet. I'm sorry,' I hesitated, unsure whether to bring it up. '...about her mum.'

'Ah, yes. Well, actually, Iona is, biologically, my niece.'

'Oh, wow.'

'She's my sister Clara's daughter. I'm a firefighter. Clara and her husband John died in a car accident. Iona was just a baby, and she was in the back, not a scratch on her, thank the Gods. I was working, and got called to the accident, obviously I had no idea Clara was involved until I arrived on the scene. I got to speak to her for a few minutes before she died. She knew John was gone, and that she wasn't going to make it so she begged me to adopt Iona. Those were her last words.'

He said this calmly, obviously a story he'd had to repeat many times. It was rehearsed, but not without feeling. My eyes had filled up with tears. I instinctively put my hand on his, feeling a spark shoot up inside me despite the horror of the story he was telling. 'Oh Finn, I'm so sorry.'

'It was tough. But I adopted Iona, and when she started talking, I told her to call me Uncle Finn. But after she started pre-school, she asked if she could call me Daddy. I guess all the kids at school had Dads and she wanted to fit in.'

'I'm sure she did, but also, you are her dad, even I could tell that from just observing you for a few moments. And you're the only parent she's known.'

'Thank you. Yes.' He swallowed, and then took another swig of beer and I removed my hand, reluctantly, from his to sip my wine.

We sat in silence for a moment, smiling sadly at each other. Thoughts swirled inside my mind about how much he'd been through, the grief. The reality of taking on someone else's child. The consequent years of bringing her up to be so confident, so sweet, brave and remarkable. I couldn't find the words to communicate how impressed I was. The server came and took our order.

'My parents always worry about it. They feel guilty and wonder if they should've taken her themselves, but they were already retired, and Dad has some health problems. Plus, I couldn't ignore Clara's wishes. The other day, Mum said I ought to be married by now, and she's worried that Clara has left me with a burden, that it's stopped me from living my life.'

'And has it?' I asked gently. 'Because it's okay to admit that.'

'Not at all! I adore Iona. It's changed just about everything in my life, but hasn't stopped me from dating plenty of women.'

Plenty. Ouch.

'Her other grandparents live nearby and they're fantastic. They help a lot with school runs and childcare. And she has a trust fund, so financially she's taken care of. I'm honoured to do it.'

'I'm sure she feels very loved.'

He swallowed hard. 'Sorry, this is a bit much isn't it? I didn't invite you here to tell you all about this. Your turn, tell me about you.'

So, I did. I told him my marriage had ended, and I'd quit my job and come to find myself on this trip. I talked about my love of Scotland so far, and how calm and centred I felt, especially outdoors.

'There's something magic about being outside, I agree. Ever since Iona could walk, we've been out and about, hiking, picnics, a bit of skiing in winter.'

'And you're a firefighter?'

As if he couldn't be any sexier, he had the obvious hero job.

'Was, actually. I've resigned. A little like you, I want to find a new calling. No idea what I'm going to do, but I've got some savings and I'm taking a few months off.'

'Well,' I said as our plates were put down in front of us. The curry looked and smelled lovely. 'Here's to healing, finding ourselves and wherever we end up next.' I held up my glass.

He gave me another of those amazing smiles and clinked his glass with mine.

'Can I just say,' he said as he picked up his cutlery. 'You're very brave. Inspiring, actually.'

It'd be nice to spend some time with this man without blushing, but my cheeks grew hot. A former firefighter who'd adopted his orphan niece found *me* inspiring? I almost laughed at him.

'I don't know, it's taken me a lot of inner work to get to this point, believe me,' I told him, honestly.

'I'm sure it has.'

I smiled and took a mouthful of curry. 'Mmm, this is so good.'

'Told you. My sister was vegetarian, so I decided to give up meat when Iona came to live with me. I thought Clara would want me to raise her veggie too.'

'Wow, that's quite the sacrifice, but impressive.'

He shrugged. 'I don't miss meat, not anymore anyway. How long have you been vegetarian?'

'Since I was old enough to cook for myself. I always loved animals, and never really enjoyed meat or fish. I'm mostly vegan but it seemed easier to be vegetarian while I travel.'

'Good for you.'

'So, you're the third friend I've made along my journey,' I told him.

'Okay, who were the first two friends?'

'Well, Iona of course.'

He smiled. 'Of course.'

'And Luna. We met in Gretna and bonded quickly. We've been speaking every day. She's psychic, wise, encouraging. She lives in Inverness and she's like my new best friend and life coach rolled into one.'

'That's cool. Psychic, you say?'

'I know, it sounds a bit out there, but she runs an esoteric shop and she's into crystals and all that. I think I could be too.'

He hesitated and I wondered what he was thinking.

'I don't think it's out there at all,' he said finally, pulling out his phone. 'I've got another friend you ought to meet. I'll text you her number, you should do a session with her.'

'A session?'

'Yeah, I'll explain, but let me have your number and then I'll send you hers.'

So, we swapped numbers (hurrah! My little heart thought). And then he shared a contact with me; Trina.

'Trina is a witch, and she likes to mend souls. You can't get more out there than that,' he said, continuing with his curry as if he'd just told me Trina could mend my car or cut my hair. 'She does all sorts, spells, crystal healing, tarot reading, the lot. I did a meditation session with her, not long after Clara passed. It was a suggestion from a woman I worked with at the time. It was transformative, so I see her regularly now. She's awesome. You know, if you're into that stuff.'

I was starting to realise that I was, or at least could be, into *that stuff*, even though I didn't understand it, yet.

'I'll give her a call, see if I can see her this week.'

'No offence taken if you don't. So, what else will you do this week?'

'There's a hill my grandad climbed, I thought I'd attempt it. It took him three hours so it can't be too impossible even though I'm not very fit. I don't mind if it takes all day.'

'Let me see.'

I pulled the journal out and found the page. 'He didn't name the hill, so I don't really know exactly where it is,' I confessed. I'd been planning on googling it to try and find something on a local walking site. 'There's a view of Loch Gynknackie and the walk starts from Kingussie.'

'Oh yeah, Iona and I have walked there, the hill is called Creag Bheag, it's a great walk, fantastic views.'

'Okay good, if Iona can walk it, I can.'

Surely, I was as fit as a five-year-old? Anxiety bounced around inside me, kids had a lot of energy and he'd mentioned they spent a lot of time outdoors.

'You can do more than you think, I reckon.' He gave me such a warm smile, and I almost believed him.

'I could come. I mean if you want some company. If you don't, that's fine...'

'I do! I'd love company. And there's less chance of me breaking an ankle and being left to die up there alone.'

He chuckled. 'Okay, it's a date.'

That evening I dreamt of snuggles in bed, and soft kisses and walks across Scottish hills covered in heather with a handsome fireman...

Chapter Nine

Nora. 1967

Life was busy; we had two small children, Tom was working hard during the week, and we had things to do around the house at the weekends; errands to run and friends to see. My in-laws visited often, or we went to them.

The years went by, yet I still stayed away from Scotland. There was no bad feeling with my family, or at least none I could detect in our letters. I spoke to my brother Mal on the phone now and then. He'd gotten married and I missed the wedding. I had a nephew, but I hadn't met him.

Happy though my married family life was, I felt a calling, a yearning to go back. Not just to see my family but to see the hills and mountains, the lochs and waterfalls, the trees that had been there long before my birth, would still be there now, and would survive me. I wanted to touch them, smell the air, feel the grass beneath my feet. I'd never regret marrying Tom, but I'd always regret leaving Scotland.

I explained all this to Tom one evening while we drank tea, after the children were in bed. I thought he'd talk about how busy he was, how long the drive would be, how much it'd cost in petrol.

Instead, he silently got up, went to our bedroom, and rummaged around for a bit, then returned with a journal.

'Remember this?' he asked, putting it in my lap.

'Of course,' I said, turning the pages and looking at the photos I'd helped him place inside.

'I love your homeland, my darling,' he said, winking at me. 'And if I could pick up our shoe business and move it up there, I would. But I can't.'

'I'm not asking to move back,' I said quietly, although the idea sounded wonderful.

'How's about a holiday then?' Tom said. 'I can take a few weeks off this summer. We shouldn't have left it so long.'

I felt overcome, unable to speak. Why hadn't we gone sooner? Excuses. Babies. Busy lives. A long journey. Silly really.

By now, Frank was five, Moira nearly three. I won't lie, the journey tried all our patience, and I pondered a few times if this would be worth it. Frank was bored and wanted to stop for a bathroom break almost every hour. We ran out of snacks, and everyone got fidgety. Moira slept half the way but wailed for a good hour in the middle. I tried singing, games, pointing out trees, sheep and hills as the landscape passed by.

We stopped at a hotel near Gretna overnight, but no one slept well. Apart from short stays at their paternal grandparents, the children hadn't been away from home much and despite being over-tired, they took a good while to settle. When they finally drifted off, Tom went down to the hotel bar and brought us up a whisky each. It might be the best drink I ever had.

The following morning we continued, going further and further north, until we arrived at the farm in Lairg around dinner time on Saturday. We were weary and desperate to get out of the car and take a big lungful of that clean Highland air I'd missed so much.

My parents and Mal came out to greet us and my mother took Moira straight from the car. As if knowing this woman loved her despite not having met her, Moira rewarded her with a big smile and a huge hug that made my eyes misty.

Frank was a little shy but soon warmed up after my dad promised a ride in a tractor. After my family gave us hugs, tea and food, I fell into bed that night, content. I was home. I took a big, deep breath and slept the best I had in forever.

It's funny. Sometimes, you just go along through life. You get up and get on with your routine. You get the jobs done; feeding the family, walking the dog, cleaning the house, and bathing your bairns. You read a book or take long walks with your husband.

But when do any of us stop and think: am I living a good life? Do I enjoy myself? Am I happy?

Well, I didn't anyway. Being back in Scotland was a wakeup call. I loved my life, and yet something was missing. I loved my children, but they didn't bring me the fulfilment I wanted. I loved my home, yet the countryside was nothing to this landscape I'd grown up in. I loved Esther and Michael and my friends, but they didn't make up for long gaps between seeing my own kin.

Uprooting our lives was out of the question; everyone was settled and Tom had his business. I knew I had to savour these moments. The journey had been well worth it for two weeks in the land that I loved, with the people who knew me best.

I helped my mother around the house, and spent time talking with her, asking her about her past and telling her about my life down south.

I went out into the fields with my father, walking the land I knew so well. He talked about sheep and grass, and I listened avidly whilst watching him with his grandchildren.

I suggested Mal and I go for long walks, which helped me get to know the adult my brother had become. I got to know my sister-in-law and played with my nephew, Neil.

I cherished every moment and vowed to visit more regularly.

And we did. We went back year after year. The journey was always long, but worth it, and it became easier as the children got older. My house, my family, the love of my life was in that small Northampton-shire village. But my soul belonged to Scotland.

Chapter Ten

Marianne

The weather was set to turn any day, so we'd agreed to meet in Kingussie at ten am and make the most of another day of sunshine. This had seemed a brilliant idea the night before, feeling lovely in the presence of this wonderful, handsome man who'd sacrificed so much for his niece. He didn't think I was weird for carrying around a piece of amethyst and he seemed to love being outdoors as much as me.

However, I had one rather big problem.

I googled it, and Creag Bheag sounded like quite a steep walk in places. I'd barely climbed many real hills; although I'd previously thought I had. However, since being in Scotland I realised the hills around my hometown were barely an incline compared to this place. I'd be out of breath, red faced and worn out within a very short space of time. Call me crazy, but this didn't seem like a good look next to a man you found extremely attractive.

Still, what could I do?

Phone Luna for advice, that's what.

'Firstly, he sounds wonderful!' she said, after listening to me for a good ten minutes.

'He is!'

'Secondly, this isn't a big deal. He lives hundreds of miles from you. He's got his own stuff going on. You're not about to marry this guy. Right?'

'Well, yes I suppose they're all good points.'

I no longer had a fixed abode and didn't know where I'd move on to after the trip, but the less I dwelled on that, the better.

'So, see him as a friend. Someone to help you challenge yourself, to help you reach a new goal. Be honest about your fitness level at the start and ask if you can pace the walk. He sounds very understanding. Go and have fun!'

'Okay,' I said, taking a deep breath. 'That makes sense. You're right.'

I remembered my thoughts around having a fling, about not looking for anything serious. I realised the universe had sent me exactly what I'd asked for. I should embrace it, have a little fun, and just enjoy his company.

'I often am right to be honest,' she said, and I could hear the smile in her voice.

'How're you today, anyway? Apart from being sick of giving me life advice.'

'Far from it, anytime. I'm good. The shop has been so busy, which is great. My kids are out of school for the summer, and my parents are helping but they're getting bored so today we're heading out for a walk near the loch.'

'Which loch is that?'

'Loch Ness.'

'Oh wonderful, enjoy. I can't wait to see you in a week or so.'

'Me too. But until then, have fun with this guy. Enjoy yourself.'

So, I got dressed, threw some snacks and water into a backpack, grabbed some blister plasters in case my new hiking boots didn't agree with me, and drove to Kingussie.

Finn was already waiting in the carpark as I pulled up. He looked so pleased to see me, I thought I might just jump on him and kiss him, right then and there.

Then I remembered that this was just a friendship, at best. Potentially, a fling, at *very* best. So, I took a breath and told my beating heart to be still and focus on the present moment.

'Hey, you,' he said, giving me a brief hug. As you might expect, he smelled amazing, a wonderful blend of sandalwood and citrus. Last night we'd shared life stories but coming face to face again in daylight felt a little surreal. He knew a lot about me, yet he was still new *to* me.

'Hey yourself,' I said. 'Now, before we start. I'm not very fit,' I said, looking at the path we were to follow. 'So, we'll need to take it slow. And I'm sorry if, by the time we reach the top, I look like a sweaty, red-faced, mess.'

'I hope you do,' he said, winking at me, 'the best view is worth the effort of the climb, and all that. And remember, I usually walk with a five-year-old, so I'm not about to set off at super-fast speed.'

'Okay, good.'

Universe, please don't let me be slower than a five-year-old child.

'How about you go first, so you can set the pace?'

Off we went. There was a well-worn path, weaving past rocks, boulders and patches of heather. Conversation was easy and natural; we spoke mostly about the landscape around us. We walked at a steady pace, and every now and then, without asking, he'd notice I was a little out of breath and stop to take a photo of the view, to sit on a boulder and offer me some water.

As we got higher, we grew warmer and pulled off our fleeces to tie around our waists. Finn was wearing a t-shirt and I tried not to let my eyes rest on his toned arms.

'We're nearly at the top!' I said, out of breath, enjoying every minute but thrilled to see we were nearly there.

'Nope, that's a false summit,' Finn corrected me. 'You'll see when we get to this craggy bit, there's a fair bit more to do.'

He was right, we reached what I'd thought was the top only to see the real top, higher up in the distance. My view had been obstructed by the craggy bit, as he called it. Surely this was a mountain, not a hill. I almost laughed at the thought of me ever trying to attempt a mountain.

Now, lovely reader, I think you and I both know that if I'd been alone, I'd have turned back at this point. Great walk, but I was exhausted. My thighs ached, and I just wanted to go back down, find a nice café and have a massive slice of cake.

But I couldn't do that, not with this handsome, kind man who'd offered to give up his day to escort me. So, on we went, slowly and surely. We talked now and then but mostly I was just trying to breathe. And then, finally, we reached the top.

I was astounded. The top opened out into a ridge and the view was spectacular in every single direction. We sat on a boulder, pulled out our lunch and ate in comfortable silence.

'I want to remember this place, this moment,' I said, taking out my phone. 'Will you take a photo with me?'

'Of course.' He got up, hand outreached for my phone.

'No,' I said, '*with* me.'

He smiled, and came and stood beside me, then leaned in to smile for the selfie. I felt myself grow warmer at his proximity.

'Send me that photo, will you?' he said, as he sat back down to finish his lunch.

I asked him about other hills and mountains he'd climbed and enjoyed hearing about all sorts of adventures; different views, changing weathers, encounters with wildlife. He'd hiked Britain's tallest mountain, Ben Nevis, and been over to the Alps and up a few mountains there, too. I was in awe. If I could magically increase 500% in fitness,

I could see myself walking up mountains regularly. The effort felt so rewarding when you reached the summit.

Another couple came along, and we said hello to them and their dog. Otherwise, we didn't see anyone.

'Is it always this quiet?' I asked Finn.

'Pretty much. The Cairngorms are vast but wild. We get tourists but it's never super busy.'

I was glad; I was falling in love with this country, and I didn't want hordes of tourists spoiling it.

The descent was much easier, although a little steep in places. We went down the other side, towards Loch Gynack, taking in the glorious views. The sun was glimmering on the water, beams of light through the clouds illuminating the trees. I loved every minute. Every point my eyes flicked to, was beautiful. I wasn't sure I'd ever felt more alive. It was like I was born to climb Scottish hills. You know, ones this size or smaller, anyway.

I stopped, around halfway down, to take a photo of the loch. Finn stood beside me.

'Quite something, isn't it?'

I looked up at him. 'Thank you for coming with me.'

He looked at me, really looked, like his eyes were studying every little part of mine. Then his eyes flicked to my lips, and I thought he was about to kiss me. I held my breath in anticipation.

'I'll make you dinner,' he said, suddenly carrying on, leaving me feeling utterly deflated. 'If you're not sick of me by the time we reach the bottom.'

'Sounds great, thanks.'

Despite the fact that this couldn't go anywhere, and the fact he had a daughter when I didn't want kids, I wasn't sure I would ever get sick of being around Finn.

As expected, I'd done a fair amount of sweating and my hair was indeed a crazy, wild mess, so I went back to my cottage to have a shower. I put on some clean clothes and just a smidge of makeup, before driving over to Finn's place. It turned out he lived about halfway between Carrbridge and Aviemore, so it took me all of 7 minutes to drive there. Just enough time to psych myself up. If this was more than friendship, then it could be some simple fun. A Scottish fling. He was child-free for a while. It'd do us good to have a bit of a flirtation. I'd let the universe decide what was best.

I was living in the moment. Honestly. I never thought about the possibility of falling for this man. Seriously, that'd be ridiculous and foolish.

It was a white stone house, with dormer windows and a sweeping driveway. There were flowers growing in the front garden, and two pairs of wellington boots upside-down on a stand outside the door: one large dark green pair and the other bright pink with yellow flowers on.

Finn opened the door, wearing a pair of dark jeans and a plain grey short-sleeved shirt. His hair still looked damp, and his eyes were as greeny-browny-hazel as ever.

'Welcome,' he said, standing aside to let me in.

The hall was filled with photo frames. Finn pointed out a picture of Clara and John with baby Iona. They looked so happy. I could see that Iona got her red hair from her dad's side.

'They made a beautiful family,' I said, my heart aching for them all.

'They did,' he said softly. He cleared his throat. 'I'll give you the grand tour,' he said, directing me through a doorway. 'So this is the kitchen, obviously.' It was modern, with white units and wooden worktops, a good size with a fair few gadgets and a circular pine dining table. There was a casserole dish in the oven.

'It smells wonderful. I see you like to cook,' I observed as I peered around at the gadgets and recipe books. 'I'm impressed.'

He shrugged. 'Thanks. I learned after I adopted Iona.'

The living room had two large, comfortable looking sofas, a big TV and several bookcases full of books. Floor to ceiling windows gave a view out to a garden, with a small decking area and then grass sloping up and away from the house. There were bushes and trees and a few flower beds.

'This is beautiful,' I told him.

'Thanks,' he said, hovering in the doorway as I looked out into the garden. 'Iona's paternal grandparents help me with the garden.'

'Sounds like they help a lot.'

'They lost their son,' he said, turning to lead me back out of the room. 'So, their granddaughter is extra special to them.'

'Of course. It's lovely they live nearby.'

'It is. Next is upstairs...' He led the way up a narrow staircase and into what was obviously Iona's bedroom.

'Oh, this is wonderful,' I said, taking it all in. The walls were painted pale blue with fluffy white clouds. The letters IONA were painted above her bed in pink, and she had a vast array of toys, books, and games. There was even a little desk for her to sit at and an artist's easel.

'She likes art?'

'She loves it, she's really good too,' he said, proudly pulling out a folder with an array of drawings and paintings.

'Wow, these are better than I could do.' I was literally astounded, this kid had talent.

'I know, right? She's incredible. Look at this one.' He pulled out a painting of a tree on a hillside. 'I told her I'd frame it.'

'And she's only, what five?'

He nodded. 'Almost six. I think she's quite advanced for her age.'

'You must be really proud.'

'I am,' he said, taking a big inhale of air. He tucked the pictures away.

'Guest room,' he pointed to a room with a double bed. 'For my parents when they visit.'

I tucked my head in. It was nicely done, in shades of dusky purple and cream.

'Then bathroom, and of course my room.'

It wasn't what I expected, which would have been a typical male bachelor's room with little personality, a dark coloured plain duvet and nothing much else. Something like Ethan had when we first met.

Finn had a large oak frame bed, and a duvet with a picture of a stag on. There were blankets thrown over a couple of cosy armchairs and plenty of cushions.

'This is so nice,' was all I could say.

He shrugged. 'I want Iona to be able to come in and hang with me in here, you know on a lazy Sunday morning or whatever.'

I went over to the window, facing the back of the house, and beyond that was a field, a hill in the distance, and many, many trees.

'It's a lovely home. Iona is very lucky to have you.'

He bit his lip. 'Thank you, that means a lot.'

We blinked at each other a few times, before he turned quickly and I followed him back down to the kitchen, where he poured me a glass of red wine.

'How's Iona getting on with your parents?'

'Good, actually. I spoke to her just now. I told her you were coming over, and she was excited about it. Probably shouldn't have said anything, she'll get her hopes up.' He turned away to check on the oven. 'I heard her telling one of her friends that she hopes I'll find a girlfriend and get married.'

'Bless her. It's nice she wants you to be happy.'

'Yes. But I'm better single. I've never wanted a serious relationship, no plans to ever get married.'

Was he trying to make it clear he wasn't interested? Message received.

'I guess it's complicated with Iona...' I didn't know what else to say.

'There are many complications,' he said, distracted by his food preparation. 'Anyway, I made it clear to Iona that we're just friends.'

I nodded. Just friends. Very clear. For the best, of course, for all of us.

However, his words were easy to forget when his actions said otherwise. He looked at me with that piercing gaze, his eyes dropping to my lips and back to my eyes again.

'Dinner is almost ready, it's a sausage and bean casserole. Veggie sausages, of course.'

'That's wonderful, thank you, it smells delicious.'

As I sat at the table, I watched him serve up, moving around the kitchen, grabbing a serving spoon and plates, and dishing up our food.

He put my plate down in front of me; sausages, peppers, mushrooms, beans, and onions in a herby sauce with a side of mash potato. 'Oh yum, it's been so long since I've had a home cooked meal.'

'I hope it's alright,' he said, handing me cutlery. 'Iona likes it.'

I took a mouthful.

'Oh, this is so good, there's so much flavour,' I said, tucking in for more. We ate in silence, glancing up at each other now and then with a smile.

'What are you up to tomorrow?' he asked as we were finishing up.

'I thought I might go to Loch Morlich,' I told him. 'There's a photo of my grandad standing on a sandy beach there.'

'Another beautiful spot. You'll love it.'

'What about you, any plans tomorrow?'

He shrugged. 'Haven't thought about it much, probably go for a walk. Maybe pick up some supplies for my trip.'

'You could come with me,' I said before thinking. 'I mean, you don't have to. But I'd appreciate the company if you'd like to go.'

He stood up and cleared our plates without answering. 'More wine?' he asked, picking up the bottle. Fair enough, three days together in a row would be a bit much.

'I'd better not, I'm driving.'

'I've got some lemonade, or juice... let me see,' he opened the fridge and I saw him hesitate. 'Or...'

'Or?'

He turned around to face me, the fridge still open behind him.

'You could stay. I mean, it'd be no trouble if you'd like more wine? In the guest room, obviously. We have spare toothbrushes. And you could borrow a t-shirt or something to wear in bed? No pressure.'

My mind thought about it quickly and decided why not? I could sit here for longer, enjoy his company and drink more wine. The only alternative was to be alone in the lovely but draughty cottage I'd rented.

'Are you sure?'

'Of course. In the morning I'll make you breakfast, and we can drive over to Loch Morlich together.'

I couldn't help but let a big smile spread over my face. 'Only if you're sure? I don't want to put you out.'

'I'd enjoy it,' he said, turning back to the fridge. He pulled out a cake.

'It's toffee, and I made custard too.'

'Mmm, sounds wonderful... You've gone to so much trouble.'

He shrugged. 'I love to cook, it's no bother.'

Dessert was, just like dinner, delicious. We moved to the living room, sitting on opposite sofas, and before I knew it, we'd opened another bottle of wine. We chatted for a while about Iona, and the local area. I told him about my life back home – without all the depressing bits. Panic-attacks, binge eating, and extreme anxiety wasn't the most fun topic of conversation with a man you like, after all.

'It's nice to have adult company,' Finn said as he sat down next to me to top up my glass.

'You don't have friends over very often?'

'I hang out with my buddies from the fire station now and then, but we just tend to go to the pub.'

'Well, I'm glad to have some company as well, I thought I'd spend the majority of this trip alone.'

'That reminds me, I wanted to talk to you about something. And you need to be totally honest.' He sat back on the same sofa I was sitting on, our legs almost touching. I didn't mind. It was easier for me to see those lovely eyes.

'I'm always totally honest.'

'Me too, good. So, I was going to start the NC500 trip tomorrow. But I'll delay a few days and we could...' he hesitated. I realised I was holding my breath. 'We could go together if you want. It might be fun to go with a friend. I don't want to take over your trip though, you're doing this whole 'find yourself' thing and you've got your grandad's diary and all that. If it's a terrible idea, just tell me and we can go separately. If I bump into you along the way, great.'

He looked nervous and tense as he waited for my reaction.

I had no idea what to say. On the one hand, if I did this, there was a good chance I'd fall for him. He was attractive, kind, and a good listener. Yet he'd made it very clear we would only be friends, and anyway I wasn't ready for a new relationship. To be a pseudo mother.

Or to be making decisions about moving here. Not to mention the fact he might not fall for me, leaving me with an unrequited, broken heart.

I should say no.

'I would love that,' I said. Because he'd asked for honesty, and I really would love it. It wasn't because I was lonely, it was because I liked his company and more of it sounded wonderful.

When he went to the bathroom, I texted Luna:

> I'm living in the now. And I think right now the universe wants me to spend more time with Finn. How are you? x

She replied straight away.

> Amazing. I'm good! Have fun :) x

I sat back and stared around the room. It was so lovely, and so tidy. I wondered if he'd rushed around cleaning before I came over, or if it was always like this. It was still very light outside, and I was standing by the window, admiring the view when he came back.

'I thought I'd text your friend Trina about doing a meditation,' I told him. 'See if she's free sometime this week. Do you fancy coming along?'

'You know what, you ought to see her on your own,' Finn said, bringing through a bottle of whisky and two glasses. 'Whisky?'

'Why not, sure.' I'd probably have a headache in the morning but who cared? I was living in the now, tipsy on wine, knocking back whisky with a handsome man. It was so far removed from my 'normal' life that I almost laughed out loud with joy.

To my disappointment, Finn left the room again but returned with two glasses of water.

'Or we'll never make it out of bed in the morning,' he said, handing me one.

I almost said 'promise?' but I stopped myself. Maybe getting drunk around my new *friend* wasn't a good idea.

We chatted about everything and anything, including Iona, his work as a firefighter, and his family. We talked about my family, including my sisters and their kids. I told him things I rarely talked about, like the time my dad left when I was a kid, and how my grandmother, Nora, died before I was born yet I felt drawn to her. I wished I'd known her.

And, eventually, with sadness, Finn pointed out it was past midnight so we meandered up to bed. I hovered awkwardly in his bedroom doorway while he found a t-shirt for me to wear.

'Thank you,' I said, taking it from him. 'Tonight's been really fun. The whole day actually.'

His eyes lingered on mine for a moment. 'For me too.'

I hesitated, biting my lip. The combination of whisky and wine had allowed me to forget why we were only going to be friends. I wanted nothing more than to push him on the bed and climb on top of him.

'Good night, then.'

'Good night,' I said, taking a deep breath and turning away. I went into the bathroom, brushed my teeth with his spare toothbrush, washed my face and took off my clothes. I was just in my knickers and his t-shirt, which was embarrassingly a little too tight for me. I slipped out of the bathroom and into the guest room, dumping my clothes on a chair in the corner.

I was just about to close the door when he appeared.

'Thank you for a lovely evening,' I said, smiling. I'd sobered up and felt uncomfortable, standing there in his t-shirt, no bra, makeup off, legs exposed.

'It was really nice.' he said. He hesitated and I was about to ask him if he needed something when he spoke again.

'Can I kiss you?' he asked quietly, his eyes full of heat.

I was in front of him within a microsecond, wrapping my arms around his neck. Our lips collided with such passion, I'm surprised they didn't burst into flames. He lifted me up and carried me to the bed. Before I knew it, the t-shirt was on the floor and his mouth was on my breasts, his hands running down my body. I let out a low moan. It'd been a long time since Ethan and I had been intimate. It'd been even longer since I'd craved a man like this. I was going to enjoy every beautiful moment. An overwhelming feeling of sexual chemistry overtook my whole being.

I pulled Finn's pyjama top over his head and almost gasped at his toned body. He trailed tiny kisses down my (completely un-toned) stomach, then pulled my underwear down slowly, staring me in the eyes, tormenting me with his gaze, full of lust. Between the weight gain, and the depression, I'd forgotten what it was like to feel beautiful, or powerful. With that look, he made me feel both. My heart swelled with gratitude that this man – this gorgeous, sexy man – could want *me*, desire *me*. Not just for this, but to offer to spend time with me, day after day during his holiday.

I sat up, tugging at his trousers, pulling them down and feeling my eyes widen at his erection. He pushed me back down and returned to kissing my belly, my hips, and then moved lower to between my legs. I wasn't sure I'd ever felt this turned on, or this darn good. It was like we were born to do this, like this man knew exactly how to get me where he wanted me to be. Within minutes I was coming in his mouth, begging him to move up, to enter me. When he did, I thought I might pass out in ecstasy. He began to drive into me, both of us moaning as he came, tipping me over the edge once again, practically screaming as I lost all control.

We laid there for a few minutes catching our breaths, with him still on top of me, his head tucked into my neck. My breasts squashed against his chest. I wrapped my arms around his back and felt a whole heap of emotion bubble up, from elation to happiness, to relief – relief that I still had this sort of erotic desire inside of me.

'Are you okay?' he whispered into my neck.

'Very much so,' I whispered back.

He sat up, looking down at me. 'I'm sorry, we didn't, you know, I should've got a condom.'

'It's okay,' I told him. 'I have a coil.'

'But still.'

I just smiled. He smiled back. Then with one, easy motion he picked me up as if he was rescuing me from a fire. A move he'd no doubt made countless times, but I giggled and enjoyed it anyway. He carried me to his bedroom, gently put me on the bed and pulled the covers over me. Then he got in at the other side.

'You're so sexy.' He pushed a strand of hair out of my face.

'Really?' I said, hardly able to believe it.

'Of course!'

'I've just... this past year or so I've put on a lot of weight.'

'Marianne, you're stunning.'

The tears sprang to my eyes again, so I moved closer and tucked my head under his chin to stop him from seeing.

That night, I slept with my head on the shoulder of a man I must not fall in love with. My arm wrapped around his torso, my left leg over his.

Universe, I thought, *you've really got me into trouble.*

Chapter Eleven

Marianne

It took me a few seconds the next morning to remember where I was. I was on my side, naked, in a strange room. My eyes opened, and I stared at the wall opposite, blinking. Then I remembered how Finn's lips felt on mine ... and my chest swelled with warmth.

Slowly, I turned over. He was asleep, on his back, his mouth open just a little.

I got up as gently as I could, snuck into the bathroom and brushed my teeth. I found my clothes. Got dressed, grabbed my phone, and went into the garden.

'Good morning my wonderful new friend,' Luna said. She sounded like she was outside.

'Hello, Lovely. Is this an okay time?'

'It's perfect timing actually, I'm just walking my dog.' I didn't even know she had a dog. I couldn't wait to see her again and immerse myself into her world for a few days. 'So how did it go last night?'

'We had sex. Amazing sex.'

'Of course you did, he's gorgeous, you're gorgeous, you obviously have chemistry.'

'Luna, he lives up here and I live... well I don't even know. And he's got a kid. And I don't want kids. And I'm freaking out!'

'Okay, first, you just had sex, you didn't elope. Take a breath.'

I did as she said. 'Okay, you're right.'

'I know I am. You're single for the first time in a long time. You should be having fun, this is healthy. Don't get so carried away thinking about anything beyond today. You need to live in the moment a little more.'

'Well,' I said, wondering how she knew me so well, so fast. 'That's true. You have a point. I'm on holiday, I should be enjoying myself.'

'Exactly! You're brave and passionate and on this adventure to find yourself. Why can't that journey involve sex with a really gorgeous man?'

I laughed. I knew I'd called Luna for exactly this talk. Nancy would've been shocked, told me this was unlike me, and then asked how long before I settled down in Scotland, married Finn and had lots of babies (she never did get why I hadn't wanted any.)

'Okay, yes, you're right. Thank you, Luna.'

'You shouldn't need me to tell you this. Have a little confidence. No shame. No *shoulds*.'

'Ah, yes,' I took a deep breath. 'Thank you.' I felt myself stand a little taller.

'So how was it?'

'What?'

'His kitchen,' she laughed, 'I'm kidding! The love making of course!'

'It was amazing,' I said, keeping my voice low. 'The best I've had. With Ethan, it was just... well, it was just sex. This was... transcendent.' I felt myself blush. Which annoyed me. Luna was right, it was healthy and wonderful that I'd had a night of passion with a very hot man. I needed to stop overthinking, stop feeling embarrassed, stop worrying about falling for him. I could do this; we could have a great time together without it meaning anything beyond fun. I glanced back at the house but there was still no sign of Finn.

'I'm so happy for you. You ought to be having the best sex of your life, you're in your prime. Wait, it's fairly early, are you still at his house?'

'I'm in his garden, he's asleep upstairs.'

'I say, go get you some more.'

I laughed, but the idea stirred up a nice wave of pleasure. 'Live in the moment, right?'

'Yes! Learn to trust your instincts. And have fun! I've got to go but call me later.'

She hung up and I stared out at the fields behind the house. She was right, of course. I should be having fun. I wasn't thinking too much about the future when I quit my job and started this trip. I was overthinking my feelings, or the potential for them to go wild. Okay, a holiday fling hadn't been on the cards when I started this trip, but surely, it could only be a good thing. A way to build my confidence while enjoying his excellent company and very hot sex.

I went back inside, then hesitated. I could go wake him, try to repeat the fun from last night. Or I could make us breakfast. My stomach groaned, making the decision for me.

My thighs ached from the mountain climb yesterday as I looked around in his kitchen cupboards. I found some porridge, which I decided to serve with banana and peanut butter. That'd do nicely.

He came down as I was stirring the pan.

'Hey,' he said, smiling from the doorway. He was in pyjamas and looked slightly awkward. I wondered for a moment if he'd rather I just left.

'Hey, sorry I'm so hungry I thought I'd make us some porridge, is that okay?'

'Yes of course, thank you. I'm starving too.'

He came over and I turned towards him. He gave me a quick kiss on the mouth and ran a hand through my hair.

'How're you feeling?'

'A little hungover,' I admitted. 'And my thighs…'

'Yeah, if you're not used to hiking, they scream at you the next day. You want to skip Loch Morlich today, and go tomorrow? I could use a lazy day if you're up for that?'

That sounded like heaven. Slicing a banana, I agreed.

'Sorry, making some assumptions there, if you'd like a day to yourself, that's of course fine.'

'Nope,' I said, living in the moment and trusting my instinct. 'I'd love a lazy day together.' I put the banana in the bowl. 'I mean, if you're happy with that?'

'Sounds good to me.'

I popped back to my rental cottage to get a few things, then returned. We watched a film. We ate. We talked. And we had delicious, sensational sex – more than once. Ethan and I had never done it more than twice in one day.

Finn and I watched about five minutes of a film before he was kissing me, and only a few minutes after that, I was tugging at his clothes. We did it twice on the sofa, and once with me bent over his dining table while our dinner burned in the oven.

Then later, in his bed, and even once more for luck, in the shower. It was like we were magnets, drawn together. The fizz of attraction always bubbled beneath the surface, whether we were just sipping tea, watching a film or washing dishes. He barely had to look at me and I'd want to jump on him. It was the most sensual, erotic day I'd ever had. I was sure my thighs would ache again tomorrow, but for very different reasons.

At 10pm, we were naked, in his bed, the TV on and he'd gone quiet for a while.

'Everything okay?' I asked.

He nodded but he was distracted so I turned the TV off.

'What's up?' I asked, pulling the duvet around me.

'I just... I think we should set some ground rules. Because you and I... I mean, this is amazing Marianne, really, this chemistry between us is just... wow.' My heart swelled.

'I'm excited about tomorrow,' he continued. 'And the road trip...'

'But?' I prompted, 'I'm sensing a 'but'?'

'There is.'

'But you have a daughter,' I offered. 'And a life here. And I have a life down south.'

Not much of a life, I reminded myself... a broken marriage, no home, no job, friends I'd drifted apart from, and an interfering family. But still. My life was there.

'Exactly. I don't want anyone to get hurt. Especially Iona. And especially you.'

'Look,' I said, taking a big deep breath. 'Let's just live for the day, shall we? Let's have fun and enjoy each other's company. No labels. No promises. Iona need not know. At the end, we say goodbye without any expectation of anything more.'

'You mean, we'll be friends... with benefits?' He winked and I couldn't help but laugh.

'Well, why not? We were talking about travelling together anyway. It would mean good company, and someone to share the driving. We could even share hotel rooms, which cuts down on the expense. Travelling buddies by day, great sex at night. I mean, it's great for me, anyway.'

He smiled at me. 'It is great. Are you sure?'

'That the sex is great? Yep, I am very sure.'

He laughed. 'It's fantastic,' he said, 'and yes we'd both save money on hotel bills and petrol.'

He didn't want a girlfriend, that much was clear. And I didn't want to be one, anyway.

This way, I'd have company for travelling, with incredible sex along the way. I'd even save a bit of money, which would come in useful when I set up home again, wherever that may be. Seeing as he wanted a change of career too, maybe we'd help each other figure it out.

What could go wrong? Worse case, I got my heart broken. It couldn't be any worse than falling out of love with your husband after ten years, the man you thought was your soul mate. A short holiday romance would be easier to get over, surely.

'Then it's a deal,' I said, tucking my head into his shoulder.

The next morning, we drove to Loch Morlich, which was even more beautiful than my grandad had described. A reddish sandy beach on the shores of a gorgeous body of water, it was lined with trees and mountain views on the horizon. We walked for a while, holding hands, and it felt nice. So very nice. We found the spot where Grandad's photo had been taken, and Finn took one of me so I could show him. We did a selfie, too and then continued our walk.

After that, Finn went grocery shopping while I went to see Trina, his witch friend. I had no idea what to expect but I was high on happy hormones and, quite honestly, felt open to anything.

Trina lived in a large house, on a single-track road, literally in the middle of nowhere. It took me a while to find it. She came out onto the drive as I was pulling up.

She had a long, flowing white dress on, lots of crystal bracelets, and big colourful earrings. Her blonde wavy hair was hanging loose around her shoulders, and she had an energy about her that oozed calm and tranquillity.

'Hello Marianne,' she said in a soft voice, holding out her hands. I put mine in hers. 'You're very welcome here.'

'Thank you,' I liked her instantly. 'I'm very glad to be here.'

'I thought as it's a nice day, we could do this in the garden,' she said, leading me around to the back of the house.

'It's such a beautiful day,' I agreed, taking it all in. She had a large lawn, with a stone firepit set up and benches around it. There were several trees, scotch pines, I think. She'd laid out a circular blanket, some cushions, and placed large crystals on the ground. There was a low table, with a small cast iron cauldron, glass water jug and two glasses. She gestured for me to sit on the blanket and poured us some water.

'So, you said you'd like to do the spiritual awakening meditation that Finn did?' she spoke as she lit a match and set light to something inside the cauldron.

'Yes please. To be honest I've no idea what to expect but he highly recommended you. What's in there?' I said, peering into the cauldron. This was weird, but good, weird. I liked it.

'Some sage and other herbs, and lavender incense. It should help cleanse and relax you.'

I had a vision of myself driving away high and stifled a giggle.

'So, what will happen, in my meditation?'

She smiled. 'It's different for everyone so I can't give you any ideas on what you'll see. Go in with an open mind and know that you're safe and supported.'

I sipped some water. The smells from the cauldron wafted towards me, and I inhaled and felt myself relax. I'd done quite a bit of meditation before, but nothing like this.

'Would you rather sit, crossed legged in a lotus position? Or lie down?'

I expected I'd fall asleep if I lied down, so I decided to sit with my legs crossed. No mean feat when you have achy thighs, but I was comfortable.

Trina told me to close my eyes, and then led me on a guided meditation. Her voice became quieter, softer, and slower. She told me to take several deep breaths and then described a white light coming down from above, and into my crown chakra. Then she talked about that thread of light healing me and connecting me down through my root chakra to the Earth.

I pictured the light, imagined it healing me; physically (my thighs were no joke), but also, mentally. Mending that broken part of me that took me to a dark place. Repairing the damage that falling out of love had done. Rebuilding my heart, my resilience, my passion to live life fully.

'Now,' said Trina gently, just as I felt myself full of light. 'Picture yourself in a wildflower meadow. There's poppies and foxgloves, primrose, and thistles. Long grasses. It's calm and peaceful. You can hear birds, a gentle breeze and the sound of water flowing in the distance. Take your time to walk around. Smell the flowers. Take a big deep breath... and exhale.'

I felt rather wonderful already. I could see vivid flowers, all those she'd described as well as cornflowers and big oxeye daisies.

'As you walk through the meadow, you come to a stream. Put your hands in the water if you like, feel the cool water, and let it cleanse you.'

I pictured myself doing just this; imagined the water healing me of the sadness I'd felt over the last year. I put my hands on my chest, imagining I was letting the water soak through my clothes and to my heart.

'Walk along the stream a little way, notice the sound of the water, and if there are any creatures around you, maybe some wildlife.'

I noticed a cat on the other side of the stream, cleaning itself. She was black and white and looked up at me for a moment. I'd wanted to adopt a cat my whole life but Mum had never agreed. Ethan was allergic, not to mention more interested in human babies than fur babies. I realised with a smile that I could do that, now. Wherever I ended up, I was rescuing a cat.

Sorry Universe, I'll focus on the meditation. Cute cat, though.

'Up ahead,' continued Trina, 'you see a wooden bridge arching up and over the river. Walk towards it, and cross over to the other side.'

I did as she said, my mind totally absorbed once again.

'You climb a gentle embankment and see a cave in the hillside. It's glinting in the sunlight. Walk towards the cave.'

'As you approach you see a bright blue light, it's ethereal, magical, and calming. Step into the cave.'

I saw the light, totally immersed in my meditative state. My human body almost felt like I was levitating; perhaps I was.

'You see a figure emerging in the light, it's one of your spirit guides. You need not be alarmed. This being loves you unconditionally. This may be someone familiar to you, a loved one who's passed. An ancestor. Or maybe even an animal. It might not look like anything you've seen before on this Earth. This being wants to connect and is providing you with healing energy. They step forward and embrace you. Now, step back. Take a seat or stand and converse with your guide. Greet them and ask them any questions you seek answers to.'

I saw a woman emerge; she felt familiar, but I didn't know who she was. She looked at me with such love I felt my eyes well up. She wore a long, pale pink dress. She had blue eyes and a kind smile.

'Marianne,' she said. 'I'm so glad you came. Would you like to ask me anything?'

I pushed aside any feelings of silliness, or scepticism. I felt fully engaged.

'Am I on the right path?' I asked inside my mind, for lack of a more original question. I'd never done anything like this before, never even considered it. But in that moment, I believed with 100% certainty that what I saw was real.

'Define what is the right path. You are here to learn, to grow, to evolve as a soul.'

'Will my current path bring me happiness?'

Because that, I realised, was what I sought. I wanted a life with simple things, a nice home in a nice place, with meaningful friendships. A job that fulfilled me and provided a sense of purpose. A cat, obviously, or maybe three. And to fall in love with the right person. Not someone who was just there, at the right moment, like Ethan had been. Someone who understood me, who shared the desire for the simple things, and who complimented the happiness I'd created for myself, but wasn't the sole source of it. To live a calm, gentle existence, enjoying things, people, and places that I loved. It didn't seem too hard to obtain and yet I'd gone through 35 years without achieving it.

'You are on the path to contentment,' said my guide. 'You're following your instincts and that's always a good thing.'

'Will Finn hurt me?' I was surprised this question came next; I was vulnerable, I knew, but I didn't want him to be at the top of my agenda.

'That is yet to be determined. Follow the path and grow into the woman you were born to be.'

'What about the future, what about when this trip is over?'

'You'll know what to do. You're a healer, Marianne. You'll help people in a similar way that Trina and Luna help people. You just need to trust, learn, and grow a little more first.'

'I understand. Is there anything else you'd like me to know?'

'You're a lightworker, Marianne.'

I had no idea what this meant, but before I could ask Trina's voice began again –

'You only have a few moments more with your guide, so don't forget to thank them, and say your goodbyes.'

I did as she said, thanking and bidding farewell to this Goddess, or Angel, or whatever she was. I felt like I'd had nowhere near enough time with this wonderful creature.

Trina led me back to the bridge, over the river, to the meadow. She said some words, something about a light council that I didn't understand. The direction of her voice was changing, and I realised she was moving around me.

'Wiggle your fingers and toes, and then open your eyes, whenever you're ready.'

I blinked, looking out at the garden, squinting in the sunshine.

Trina told me she'd balanced out my chakras; that my heart chakra, in particular, needed work and told me how to work on this myself. She told me my guide is always with me, and I can access her at any time. She encouraged me to drink a glass of water. I listened, in a bit of a daze, taking it all in.

'Do you know what a lightworker is?' I asked, wondering if my imagination had made it all up. Ethan would laugh hard if I told him about this.

Trina smiled. 'A lightworker is someone who feels the call to help others. It might be through work, say a teacher, a doctor or a vet.

Or maybe through motivational speaking or writing. Maybe even just carrying out random acts of kindness.'

'Wow, okay. That sounds... kind of wonderful.'

'It is. Google it, when you're ready. Today, just take some time to process and make sure you keep hydrated.'

'Thank you.'

She pressed something into my hand. 'White heather, for good fortune.'

I took the small, tied bundle and thanked her. As I drove away, I felt cleansed and in a way I couldn't explain, as though part of me was healed.

I returned to my rented cottage, processing what I'd experienced while I gathered up the rest of my things. Finn had suggested I take everything to his place before we set off for the NC500.

Waiting for me at the cottage was a special delivery parcel from Aunt Moira, which I scooped up and took with me.

'So, how was it?' asked Finn after he'd helped me unload my bags. We were sitting in his kitchen with a nice cup of jasmine tea.

I told him all about it, and he just listened, nodding occasionally, and smiling. 'Amazing, isn't it?'

'Yes, so you've got a spirit guide?'

'Yep. I've got two, one is a stag. And then I also have Quinn. He's a wise old man, who always shows up in dungarees. He gives me guidance, and comfort.'

He glanced at me. 'Sorry, I know it's a bit woo woo.'

'Not at all, well maybe yes, but I don't mind woo woo,' I felt quite the opposite in fact. I decided it was time I embraced "woo woo".

I told him about the woman I'd seen in my meditation, and some of what she'd said. He listened intently, asking questions, and taking me seriously. Then he sent me a link to a guided meditation, so that

I could connect with my guide again sometime. I floated around the rest of the evening as we made a pasta dish together and shared it with a glass of delicious red wine in front of a log fire; it'd turned quite cool.

We were looking over a map of the NC500 and comparing it to Grandad's route, when I remembered I hadn't opened my parcel from Aunt Moira.

Inside was a note, sending me her best wishes. There was a small ring box.

'Grandad wanted you to have this, and as I've no daughters, who better to give it to? It was your Grandmother Nora's ring.'

I opened the box to find a beautiful gold ring, recently cleaned by the look of it, with tiny emeralds inlaid around a small diamond. I slipped it on my right-hand ring finger and ran my thumb over it.

'How special.' I showed it to Finn.

Moira's note also read -

"There's also a bunch of photos, I had some copies made. I wrote on the back who's who."

Finn and I went through the photos together. There were a bunch more of Grandad on this trip, including with my grandmother Nora when he met her in the highlands.

I froze when I got to one of the photos, my eyes filling up with tears and spilling over before I had time to check myself.

'What is it?' Finn said, sitting up concerned.

'This is the woman I saw,' I whispered. 'In the crystal cave.'

'Maybe you've seen this photo before,' he said.

'I definitely haven't, I'd remember.'

'And you're sure this is the woman you saw?'

'One hundred percent.'

I turned the photo over. On the back, Aunt Moira had written:

Beatrice Forester, your great-grandmother. Circa 1960. We called her Nana Bea.

Chapter Twelve

Nora. 1970

Ten years I'd spent with Tom. Ten happy years before we faced our first real hurdle. Of course, it'd been hard when Frank came along. And I'd had my moments, times where I missed Scotland with a physical ache and even felt a little resentful. Moments when Tom was very stressed with work and had been a little sharp with me. Just life's normal ups and downs.

But mostly we were content, happy, even more in love than when we'd first met.

And then, one day, things changed. It literally happened overnight.

It was September 1970. Moira started at the village school. She looked so beautiful as we walked from our door to the gates. She skipped along in her little grey dress, hair in plaits, excited to begin her day. She wasn't one of those children who'd cry easily. She was a tough, strong girl, just as willing to climb a tree or help Tom with fixing his car as Frank was.

I watched her walk away from me, and I went home. I tidied up a little.

And then it hit me.

Between the hours of 9 and 3, I was superfluous. Yes, I could idle myself cleaning the house, preparing food, mending clothes. I always had errands to run and things to do.

I was bored. I could pop out and see a friend or my dear mother-in-law, Esther, but that was about as much variety as I got. I considered returning to my previous job, at the haberdashery shop, but even that idea didn't appeal.

For three, hard long months, I mooched around, unsatisfied without any ideas for a cure. I was a little cold and distant with Tom.

It was a few days before Christmas when he asked me what was wrong. The children were out with their grandparents, and I was wrapping gifts.

'Nothing. Away with ye,' I said, forcing a smile.

'It's not nothing, my darling,' he said, sighing and sitting opposite me at our dining table. 'You've not been yourself for months.'

I stayed silent. Partly because I didn't know how to explain myself.

'You've nothing to say, then?' he asked, his tone less friendly.

Stubborn, I shrugged. He left me be. Christmas came and went. Tom started working more, and I couldn't blame him. I was a sullen, grumpy thing.

It was only one day, while I was staring out at a tree in our garden and contemplating what was wrong, that I feared I'd lose him. There had to be attractive young women at work, in fact I'd met a few of them. What if some young, fun, beautiful creature tempted him away? I had to pull myself together, or risk losing the best man I'd ever known.

I had a friend, Beth. She lived next door and had two little ones of her own. We often spent time together, but we'd never really spoken about anything important, deep, or meaningful. It was always about the kids, or a recipe, or the weather, or occasionally we'd swap books to read.

A little unusual; she had a crystal ball and read tea leaves. She had tarot cards and made her own herbal remedies (which I admit worked wonders whenever one of my bairns had a fever). I'd seen her staring up at the moon, whispering. And on Halloween, she created a little altar in her house to honour her dead ancestors.

I found her a little eccentric, but always kind and thoughtful. She was right next door, and I needed a female chat.

I invited her to my kitchen, and, over tea and biscuits, confided how unhappy I was. I didn't really understand why, and I had no clue what to do about it. I admitted I'd been distant with Tom, that we'd barely spoken or been intimate in months.

'You need a hobby,' she said, watching me with sympathetic eyes as I tried to hold back tears. 'Or a job. Something that lights you up, brings you fulfilment.'

'You're right,' I said, realising it was obvious. 'I wasn't built to be a housewife.'

'You're a great mother,' she flattered me. I was only average, and that was fine. I did my best, but I wasn't naturally maternal. 'But,' she continued, 'you need something for you.'

I sighed. 'I am skilled at nothing!' I said, sitting down opposite her to sip my tea.

'You can learn a skill.'

'In what?'

'What have you always wanted to learn about?'

'I've no idea.'

'I could do a reading,' she offered. 'With my tarot cards. Or get my crystal ball.'

'Thank you,' I said, offering her another biscuit. 'But I think I have to figure this out for myself.' Partly because the cards scared me, to be honest.

We discussed ideas. Before she left, she encouraged me to talk to Tom.

So, the following Sunday morning, I arranged for the children to spend the day with Beth. They were delighted; they loved Beth and her two kids.

'Can we talk?' I asked Tom after he'd come back from walking the dog.

'I'd like that,' he said kindly.

'I've been unhappy,' I admitted. It felt better just to say it out loud.

'I know. I don't know why. You won't talk to me.'

'I'm talking now,' I snapped. He sighed but waited for more.

'I'm bored, Tom. I'm so, so very bored.'

He gave a little laugh.

'What's funny?'

'Nothing, it's just I'm so busy, I hardly have enough hours in the day, and here you are, bored. We have the opposite problem.'

'Yes. Well. I think I need a job.'

'Okay.'

'I'm sorry. I'm sorry I've been difficult to live with.'

'Do you resent me?' he asked quietly.

'What? No!'

'I think you do,' he said sadly.

'For what?'

'I created this life. I determined we had to live in England. I took you away from the place you love.'

I realised he was right. I did resent him, just a little.

'It's not your fault, I was a willing participant, and I still love you and adore our children.'

'But it's not enough?'

'I need something more.'

'More and more married women are going to work these days. So do it.'

'But do what, I've no clue.'

'You liked working at the fabric shop, before the children.'

I shrugged. 'It was okay.'

'Well what interests you?'

We talked for a while about what I liked. I obviously loved my children; but I didn't want to work with other people's kids. Sewing; but no, I didn't want to be a seamstress. On and on we went.

When, finally, I knew.

I wanted to bake.

Tom was supportive. Esther and Michael helped with the children when needed. I took some classes. I worked a few days a week in a bakery. And then I undertook my first commission; a child's birthday cake, with a football theme. It was a thing of beauty, even if I do say so myself.

I started a business, and it grew.

Within the next few years, I was making cakes, bread, scones, pastries and all sorts. For all occasions from christenings and weddings to corporate celebrations. Some of my goods were served in the local café. I had to take on an assistant.

I loved baking, but I particularly loved cake decoration. The creativity, the intricate details, the joy of seeing someone's face light up when I created a personalised cake just for them.

I was a wife and mother but I also had something just for me. Something that made me feel whole.

The local newspaper called me a *businesswoman*. I had found my calling. I was flying high.

Chapter Thirteen

Marianne

My human brain, which up until now had been fairly logical, couldn't really process the meditation nor the photograph of Beatrice. I called Luna, of course, who talked about spiritual awakenings and Bea watching over me and guiding me. It was both wonderful and, honestly, a little weird.

Finn thought it was cool but didn't freak out. He told me he'd share his own experiences with Trina when we were travelling. We spent the next day stocking up on road trip snacks and planning the first leg of our North Coast 500 route, which would take us further north to Inverness, then up the east coast to John O'Groats.

I wasn't sure I'd been this excited in years, following the same path as Grandad Tom's journey, seeing new places... and of course spending time with my new friend, Finn.

He had a better and bigger car than me, so we agreed to leave mine at his place and do a circular route. I'd come back to his house to collect it when we were done. This meant I was 'stuck' with him for the whole trip. I couldn't change my mind and head back easily, or decide to go off on my own. I didn't think that was likely, and I couldn't think of any other way unless we drove in separate cars, which made no sense.

As Luna said, worst case scenario, I'd hire a car and go off on my own.

On our last afternoon before we set off, we went to Loch an Eilein for my final Cairngorms walk. I'd barely scratched the surface of Britain's largest national park, and I knew I'd have to come back. Below wet and drizzly grey skies, we enjoyed a walk among pine trees and along gorgeous shores. Once again I felt my heart lift at the beautiful landscape. I realised with a smile that I'd rather be here, by this loch, in the rain, than in the sunshine anywhere else.

Finn and I talked about everything and anything. It didn't feel like a new relationship; it felt like I'd known him for a long time. But also; the fact this couldn't become serious made me feel relaxed, open, and able to enjoy the moment. Finally.

The next morning, we bundled our array of clothes, walking gear, snacks, and everything else we would (and probably wouldn't) need into the car. I loved the Cairngorms, but it felt good to be on the road again, this time with a lovely companion. I couldn't quite figure out how it'd happened, but I also couldn't imagine continuing the trip without him.

On the way, we detoured slightly to Culloden Moor. Grandad hadn't been, but Finn mentioned that he'd always wanted to go. I was keen to see as much of Scotland as I could, so we stopped for a few hours.

The Battle of Culloden site is both beautiful and poignant. We were both quiet as we walked around, reading about the final battle of the Jacobite rising in 1746, pausing at each of the memorial stones etched with the names of those who had fought, bled and died. It was windy and grey, and a few times I took a moment to stop and look out over the site, feeling the breeze whip up my hair as I tried to imagine the horrors, the bloodshed, the loss, and death.

Finn stopped by a stone marked Clan Mackintosh, kneeled, and put his hand on the top. I realised I didn't even know his last name.

'You're a Mackintosh?' I asked him softly.

'I am,' he nodded. 'I don't know much about my ancestors, really. I should ask my dad.'

'My grandmother's maiden name was Lindsay,' I told him. I'd seen lots of Lindsay Clan items in the gift shops during my trip and bought a Lindsay tartan scarf for the winter. I knew very little about the family history, but liked the idea that I was a descendant of a Scottish clan.

'So, you're a true Scot then,' he said quietly, as he stood again. 'You belong here, for sure.'

I smiled and squeezed his hand as he looked down at his clan stone.

'I feel an overwhelming sadness here,' I said.

'Me too,' he said, squeezing my hand back.

We spent over an hour wandering around and enjoyed a cup of tea in the café. We used our phones to read more about our respective clans, and their contribution to Scottish history. I wondered if this was why the land had called to me, why I felt so grounded here... I was of Scottish blood.

A few hours later, Luna was putting a blue crystal bracelet on my wrist, after greeting me with an enormous, tight hug.

'Lapis Lazuli,' she said as she rolled the elastic over my hand. 'It's good for communication, the perfect friendship bracelet.'

'I love it, thank you.'

She greeted Finn with the same warmth, delighted to meet him and winking at me over his shoulder as they hugged.

Her shop was wonderful. She stocked everything you might imagine and more, from crystals and incense to cast-iron cauldrons and tarot cards. I spent a good ten minutes just looking through the selection of books, and she recommended a few that might help with my 'spiritual awakening' as she called it. I was already evolving and changing, and this felt like the perfect add-on to my mental health journey over the past year. I could happily have spent hours in the shop.

I picked up a few crystals, including a piece of selenite carved into a moon shape with stars etched into it. Luna said it was for cleansing and amplifying energy, and I nodded as if I knew what this meant. The other was a small green aventurine tower, which she said would help me to manifest my desires. If I ever figured out what my desires were, that'd come in handy then. She shoved a crystal book on the pile and insisted I only pay for it at cost.

Finn found a rose quartz heart for Iona and a book about unicorns. After our retail therapy, we wandered around Inverness for a while before joining Luna and her family at their home on the outskirts of town.

I so enjoyed getting to see her world. I played with the children and read them a bedtime story, then we adults sat in the garden around a fire pit, drinking – wine for us ladies and whisky for the men. It was lush to be around people I liked so much; easy, comforting and just what my soul needed.

Her husband, Callum, was laid-back and friendly with a big beard and a colourful poncho. He fell into easy conversation with Finn, giving me and Luna the chance to talk together. It felt like I'd known her far longer than I had; we'd spoken on the phone most days in the two weeks since I met her in Gretna. Being together face to face felt a little strange at first; I'd told her so much about myself, learned so much about her, and yet we'd spent very little time in the same room. We fell into easy conversation though, and within a short space of time, I felt comfortable and familiar again.

As before, we chatted about everything and anything; sharing stories, getting to know each other even better. I was aware that our friendship so far had consisted of Luna counselling me, so I took the opportunity to learn more about her, asking questions and hearing tales about her life.

'I love how light it is here in the evenings,' I said, looking up at the sky. It was past 10pm and still bright.

'Me too,' said Luna. 'We get more than our fair share of harsh weather, but on a dry summer day, you wouldn't want to be anywhere else.'

I couldn't agree more. To think I could have gone on one of Ethan's tropical holidays instead; I'm sure everywhere he suggested was lovely, but this... This was magical. Wonderful. This was where I ought to be. This felt like *home*.

I'd been fine, growing up in Leicestershire, spending time at both of my parent's homes. I'd been okay as an adult there, too. But I'd never quite felt like I belonged. I realised it'd be hard to leave Scotland. I decided then and there, silently, that I'd start considering which of the many places I'd seen, (and was yet to see), might be a place to set up home. The idea thrilled and terrified me at the same time, but I couldn't imagine feeling content living anywhere else.

'Now,' she said after refilling our glasses and throwing an incense cone on the fire pit, which sent gorgeous smells out into the air. 'Your Nana Bea.'

'I don't even know what to think,' I said, sipping my wine. 'It's both crazy and wonderful in equal measures.' I took the photo out of my bag to show her, and she studied Bea's face.

'Wonderful. Spirit guides come in many forms,' she told me, squeezing my arm. 'Ancestors are quite common, I believe.'

'It's just... I wouldn't believe it if I hadn't seen it. You know?' I put my hands on my new bracelet, touching each of the beads in turn. Somehow, touching it grounded me, made me feel more tethered to Earth, despite this strange conversation.

'I get it. You're at the start of a wonderful journey, Marianne. I'm going to teach you about moon cycles and magic and all sorts. I don't think it was a coincidence that you met me, or Finn, or Trina. We were meant to help you on this journey of self-discovery.'

'I do feel like I was meant to meet you,' I said, squeezing her arm. 'It's just all a bit surreal.'

'Okay,' she said, sensing my need to go slow with this. 'Enough with the deep soul stuff, for now. Tell me more about Grandad Tom.'

So, I did. She was so interested that I got the journal out of my bag, and we leafed through it together, noting sweet things he'd said about meeting Nora.

'I'm going to walk into town for more wine,' Callum said, collecting up our empty bottles.

'I'll come with you,' Finn said, winking at me and squeezing my shoulder as he went by.

'Okay,' Luna said, sitting upright the moment they'd gone. 'Finn. Tell me everything. You seem very happy.'

'He's great Luna, I'm doing as you said and living for the moment. For the record, we're just friends.'

'Friends who shag!' She giggled and I couldn't help but giggle too.

'It feels weird, being with someone else. Yet I've barely thought of my estranged husband.'

She nodded. 'Have you heard from him?'

'Ethan? No. I didn't expect to.'

'What went wrong with you two?'

'I think we both fell into a relationship without thinking about what we really wanted. That was okay for a while, until we started to take each other for granted,' I admitted. 'He'd never have come here, and he'd laugh at all this spiritual stuff. He's a nice man and we had a nice marriage. But I want more than nice, I want awesome. I want a great life, in a great place, doing a great job. With a great relationship.'

'Like in the Cairngorms, with a hunky fireman and a sweet little girl?'

I rolled my eyes. 'Just friends, remember. And he isn't a fireman anymore. He's looking for a new direction. Just like me.'

'I'm sure you'll help each other to grow, whatever happens. Keep an open mind about him, though.' Luna put her hand on mine and squeezed it. 'I have a feeling he's going to be important.'

I just smiled. He was already important, but he was only going to be a chapter of my story. I knew that, and it was fine. I wouldn't allow myself to think about Finn in any serious romantic way because it'd never work with us long-term.

I asked her to tell me how she met Callum. It was a story involving a beach, some shells, a storm, and a very happy ending.

It was the early hours by the time we went to bed. Finn and I sleepily pulled the covers over us in the guest bedroom.

'I really like them,' he said quietly as I closed my eyes. 'What a great evening.'

I couldn't agree more.

Weary, and if I'm honest, a little hungover, we all ventured out to Loch Ness after breakfast for a walk. No sign of the monster, although the kids assured me that Nessie is real.

'Keep messaging me, and calling,' Luna said, hugging me tight later that day, as we prepared to leave. I felt emotional, saying goodbye with no idea when I'd see her next. 'You're fast becoming my best friend.'

'Oh, you too, and you'll come visit me, wherever I end up?'

'Of course!'

She pressed another crystal into my hand. It was a heart, sky blue, beautiful. 'Angelite. It's good for spiritual growth.'

'Thank you.' I threw my arms around her. 'For this, and everything.'

She hugged Finn, and I hugged Callum, and then we were off on our adventure.

'I just love them,' Finn said as I waved, and we drove away. 'What a nice couple.'

'I know. They're great.'

'Callum and I swapped numbers.'

'That's nice,' I wasn't surprised. Their bromance had been brewing since their second drink, if not before.

'They seem so together, so on the same wavelength, you know?' He said, smiling as he drove. 'They seem so grounded and happy.'

'You sound jealous.'

He shrugged. 'Maybe I am a bit. I've never been in love before.'

'Really?' I found it hard to believe no one had ever been in love with him.

'I've had relationships, of course, but never anything serious. It's complicated with Iona and if any woman I date shows me any hint of it being more than a fling, I walk away.'

'I can understand that,' I said. *I want the same thing*, I thought, remembering my plan to only have flings and not fall in love again. My battered heart couldn't take another breakup.

'Also,' said Finn, 'I've never really clicked with someone on a deep level, until now.'

Until now. His face flushed a little. For the first time, there was a weird silence between us. My mind went into overdrive trying to decide what those words meant and how I felt about them.

'Anyway, what about you? Fallen in love a lot?' he said suddenly. 'Apart from your husband, of course.' He laughed awkwardly.

'I had a few relationships before him, but nothing too serious. Ethan and I were in love, at the beginning. Or so I thought, now I wonder if it was just lust and the idea of being in love, rather than a meaningful connection with each other.'

'How did you meet?'

'At a friend's party. He was handsome and charming and asked me on a date. I think we just went through the motions, you know, dating for a year, moving in together. Getting married seemed the obvious next step and I never stopped to intentionally think about what I wanted my life to look like, or what sort of relationship I wanted.'

'And when you did?'

'I had some quite serious mental health problems last year,' I told him, glancing to see his reaction but his face was blank as he watched the road. 'I ended up getting some therapy, and it really made me reflect on my life. I realised we wanted different things.'

'I'm sorry to hear you had a tough time,' he said, glancing at me. 'But it's great you got some help.'

'Thank you. It took me a while to sort myself out. Ethan wasn't always very supportive, I guess that's another reason we drifted apart. Sometimes though, I think of our wedding day and can hardly believe how we've ended up.'

'Did you have a big wedding?'

'Medium, I suppose but too big for our budget,' I admitted. 'It cost a fortune, and we spent five years paying off a loan.'

'Blimey. Five years?'

'Yep. Madness. To think what we could have spent that money on.'

'Well, I suppose you thought your marriage would be forever at the time.'

'Yes, the marriage. But the wedding was just one day. We could have had a smaller wedding and gone travelling. Had a long honeymoon and several days of memories instead of just one.'

'I've always wanted to travel more too. Iona is still young, but I hope to take her to lots of different places as she grows up. If I can find a good job again.'

'Why did you quit?'

He hesitated for a moment, and I wondered if he'd want to share.

'We don't have to talk about it, if you don't want to.'

'No, it's fine,' he began. 'A year ago, I got injured on the job, fractured a few ribs and broke my right leg. It was an awful night. A child died in my arms.'

I gasped and put my hand on his thigh. 'I'm so sorry Finn.'

He shook his head. 'It's okay. I had a lot of counselling, and I recovered physically but I struggled for a while. They let me take quite a bit of time off, but I realised I didn't want to go back. Not out of fear, or trauma. I just realised it wasn't the right fit for me anymore. The shift patterns were always tricky with Iona. Her grandparents help a lot, but they're not getting any younger and I've enjoyed being at home with her more. I've got some savings so I'm taking some time out. I'm hoping this summer I'll have an epiphany and work out what I want to do next.'

'You've gone through a lot,' I said, removing my hand from his thigh and squeezing his arm gently. 'It's no wonder you want to start afresh.'

'Also,' he said, scratching his chin, 'it's a high-risk job, you know? I thought about what would happen to Iona if something happened to me. She doesn't have any other aunts or uncles, and her grandparents are all that bit older. I loved it for many years, but it's time to do something else.'

It had been easy to picture the hero, running into a burning building or rescuing someone from a crushed-up car. I hadn't thought much about the horrors he'd seen, the personal loss he'd witnessed with his sister, and the risks he'd taken to help others. I had a newfound respect for him.

'That makes sense,' I said, trying to wipe the image from my head of him holding a dying child. 'I think you're amazing,' I said, and he shook his head a little. 'No, I mean it. You chose a career that's incredibly brave.'

'And yet now I'm quitting.'

'I think it takes courage and a lot of self-awareness to find a new path.'

He smiled at me. 'Thank you. What about you, what are you going to do when this trip is finished?'

'I have no bloody clue,' I said, looking out at the passing views. 'I guess I'm looking for an epiphany too.'

We drove over the Dornoch Firth Bridge, and headed into Golspie, a small town on the coast. We got some delicious, hot chips, crisp on the outside, fluffy on the inside, and ate them on the beach. I took my shoes off and let the sand filter between my toes.

'Ah this feels so good, we're on holiday properly now,' I said, watching the waves roll on the shore.

Finn put his rubbish to one side and laid back on the sand. I lay back beside him, and his hand found mine.

'I'm glad I met you,' he said quietly. I turned my head towards his.

'I'm glad I met you too. Maybe we're supposed to heal each other a bit.'

He turned his head too, so our faces were inches apart.

'I think you're already healing me,' he said, lifting our locked hands to kiss mine gently.

See. Just friends. You know, with benefits.

We checked into a hotel, and he was pulling my clothes off as soon as we got to the room. He pushed me up against the wall, kissing my neck. I tugged at his clothes, and before I knew it, we were having hot, fast sex against the wall.

'We couldn't even make it to the bed,' he said, grinning as we finished, my blood pulsing around me in euphoria. I giggled. I'd been crazy about Ethan once, it was true. But the sex had been nothing like this. Never this hot, this passionate, this intense.

I was going to miss it, when we parted ways, I realised.

Best to make the most of it now, then, I decided.

So, we did it again that night. Three times, in fact.

Did I mention the sexual chemistry between us was amazing?

Chapter Fourteen

Marianne

'Hi, Chum,' I whispered sleepily when I woke up the next morning and found Finn looking at me.

'Hi, Pal.' He grinned, kissed me on the forehead and sat up. He walked naked to the shower. Blimey, he was so good to look at.

I sat up, stretched, and thought about the day ahead; we were driving up the coast to John O'Groats and I was rather excited about it. I picked up Grandad's journal and flicked through the pages on this section. He'd written about lovely beaches and spotting different sea birds. He'd even seen seals. He wrote that reaching JOG (how he referred to John O' Groats) felt like reaching the top of the world. He never expected to leave Britain, so I suppose it was. It turned out he travelled on many holidays with my Auntie Moira; she took him wherever she went. I liked thinking about the young Tom, completely unaware that he was about to fall in love. Or that he'd ever fly on a plane someplace far away. It somehow made me feel better. I, too, had no idea what the future would hold. But for the first time in a while, I knew it'd work out okay.

We had a quick breakfast and hit the road, me driving this time. The landscape was fairly flat, and the roads quiet and easy to navigate. We could see the sea almost the whole way. The universe blessed us with blue, sunny skies and it was warm and bright.

Finn called Iona while I drove, I could hear her cute sing-song voice on the other end of the line.

'Hello, my wee lass. How're you doing?'

'Hi Daddy! I'm okay, we went to the park, and I met a very cute nice dog. Can we get a dog?'

'Dogs take a lot of work; you have to walk them every day.'

'That's okay, we like walking.'

'And you have to pick up their poo.'

'You can do that.'

'So can you.'

'I suppose.'

'Let's talk about it when we get home.'

'Where are you now Daddy?'

'I'm on the little holiday I told you about, where I drive about for a while seeing different places.'

'But you must not drive and talk on the phone at the same time.'

'That's true.'

'Well, who is driving then, I can hear the car?'

Gosh, not much got past this kid. I smiled.

'Marianne,' he said, surprising me.

'You're still with her? I really like Marianne.'

'Yes, I like her too.'

'Daddy?'

'Yes Iona.'

'Is Marianne going to be your girlfriend?'

I kept my eyes on the road. This is why he wasn't going to tell her, I thought.

'No, we're just friends.'

'Okay. I'm going to go play now. Byeeee!'

'Bye, wee Hen.'

He exchanged a few words with his Mum, and I focused on the road.

'Iona sounded full of beans,' I said, after he'd ended the call. We were pulling off, down a narrow road leading to a beach.

'She always is, my little ray of sunshine,' he said, smiling.

'You don't talk about her that much.'

He hesitated, thinking about his words.

'I suppose I'm trying to keep my normal 'dad' life separate from this little holiday bubble. I adore her, but it's nice not to think about unicorns and art supplies and laundry and all the other parenting duties while I'm here with you.'

'I get that.'

'Wow, we're at Keiss Beach already?'

'We sure are.'

It was beautiful; golden sands curving around a gorgeous crescent bay. It was the perfect place to eat the picnic we'd picked up enroute. Finn kept a couple of camping chairs in his boot, so we folded them out and sat near the shoreline, watching the waves gently rolling in and out.

'Take a big breath of that fresh sea air,' I said, closing my eyes and breathing it in deep through my nose.

'Wonderful, isn't it?' Finn took his shoes off and dug his toes into the sand. I decided to do the same.

'I can't tell you how good this trip has been for my mental health,' I said, opening my eyes again. 'As good as therapy.'

'I agree. I forgot you said you had some counselling last year.'

'Yes. I'm afraid I'm a work in progress.'

'Aren't we all?'

'True enough.'

I wanted to remember everything; this beautiful place, the sound of the waves, the colour of the sand, the smell of the sea... and most importantly, this relaxed feeling. And of course, this lovely, kind, calm man who I could just be myself with. Some day, when I was inevitably stressed or unhappy, I'd take myself back to this place in my mind. I'd remember this day, take a big breath, and transport my thoughts back to this very moment.

We were quiet for a while, watching the waves, nibbling our food. I tried to commit as many details as I could to my memory.

'So, tell me to mind my own business if you like,' Finn started. I couldn't imagine he could ask anything I wasn't happy to talk about.

'Okay...'

'What went wrong with you and Ethan?'

'Ah.' I was happy to share. Maybe it'd do me good. I told him the same story I'd told Luna; how we'd taken each other for granted, didn't have much fun, and drifted apart.

'I realised we wanted different things,' I continued, as I stared at the water. 'He wants to go on package holidays and lay in the sun. I want to do road trips like this one. He wants to have kids, I don't. But it wasn't just the big things; we had different interests, different hobbies. I don't know if we ever really had a lot in common but last year, I really noticed it. What with my mental health issues, and him bringing up the baby issue all the time, it just created this giant chasm.'

I glanced away from the sea and at Finn, who was staring at me intently.

'You don't want kids?' he asked quietly, looking away.

'No,' I said, taking a deep breath. It shouldn't matter, we were only friends. 'I've never wanted them. I made it really clear to Ethan before we got married but he was convinced I'd change my mind, that my clock would start to tick, or whatever. I didn't change my mind, though.'

'The clock hasn't started ticking?'

'Nope. And you know what, I've read a lot about this. Women are expected to be desperate to become a mother, and a lot of us just don't feel that way. Then we're deemed selfish or abnormal.'

'I don't think it's selfish,' Finn said, but he didn't look at me. Something had changed and I didn't want to think about why. 'It just means it's not for you.'

'Thank you, but you wouldn't believe the comments I've had. People tell me I'm good with my niece and nephews, over and over. My mother once said to me *you'll be a wonderful mother when you finally decide to have kids...*' like it was an inevitability that I'd change my mind. No one in my family seems to get it.'

'Most people have trouble understanding other people's life choices.'

'Exactly. It's not as if I don't love children. I adore my nieces and nephews. I enjoyed our time with Luna's kids. I just don't see myself having one of my own. I'd rather adopt a cat. In fact, I'm going to as soon as I get settled somewhere.'

Finn just nodded. He was staring out to sea, thinking.

Was he thinking about me, about us? If he had any thoughts about us becoming a real couple, was he now thinking about how we wouldn't have biological children? That Iona wouldn't have a sibling?

I told myself to stop being stupid. It was irrelevant, of course. We were only friends. He'd made that very clear.

'You okay?' I asked him after a few minutes.

'Yeah, sorry. So, Ethan wants kids then?'

'Yes, he does. It's not the only reason we split up, but I think it would have become a big problem if I didn't give in and change my mind.'

'Do you think you ever will? Change your mind, I mean.'

'No,' I said firmly. 'I'm certain. I don't ever want to have a baby.'

'Fair enough,' he said. There were many words he didn't say, and that was fine, too.

Maybe this would help him, or both of us, keep firmly in the friendzone. He clearly had an issue with it and we could never be a real couple if we wanted different things.

Would it always be this way, I wondered? Was I going to have to mention this upfront with every man I dated? What would be the point of starting something with someone, developing deep feelings, then having to tell them further down the line. It could potentially cause a lot of pain. Surely, I'd have to tell anyone I met upfront. Why did things have to be so complicated? I decided I'd worry about it later.

We were silent for a while and then he suggested we do a guided meditation. The beach was empty, and we both had our wireless earbuds, so he sent me a link.

With the sound of the waves in the background, I settled back and listened to a soothing male voice guide me through a chakra-balancing meditation. I didn't fully understand chakras, nor did I understand everything that was being said, but I felt re-energised, calm and content by the time it was finished.

I blinked a few times as it came to an end, squinting in the sunlight. Finn was staring at me.

'You okay?' he said, smiling.

'Yes. How about you?'

'Yep. I'm good.'

'That was wonderful. Thank you for introducing me to this stuff.'

'I'm just glad you don't think I'm crazy,' he said.

'Not at all. I'm loving it. I feel more connected to... well I don't know what, the universe? The divine? The Earth. Everything.' I almost added 'and you' but stopped myself.

He smiled. 'I always get this strong sense of connection, of unconditional love and support. Whether it's grounding to Mother Earth, or connecting to some sort of deity, I don't know. I don't think we're supposed to know, but it feels good and anything that's good for mental health is something to do often.'

'I agree.'

We were quiet for a while, looking out at the waves. I kept wondering what he was thinking. Why had the conversation about kids bothered him? Did he want to have more children? I knew I couldn't change myself for anyone, I'd almost done that with Ethan. I had to continue to find myself, and my own path, before thinking about a relationship. I glanced at him. The realisation hit me that I had already gone past the friend zone with Finn. Perhaps it should have been obvious but I must have been in denial until that point.

However, I decided that not every relationship had to end in marriage and happily ever after. This could be a wonderfully healing relationship, where we both achieve personal growth, have some fun and enjoy some incredible sex. Maybe that was all we needed right now. It didn't have to be any more than that. I felt lighter, more self-aware and had greater clarity than I had for a long time. It felt good.

This wonderful moment, on a gorgeous beach. Cool but sunny. Handsome man. In Scotland, the place that'd called me for so long. My spiritual home. I felt the happiest I had in years.

We packed up our stuff and got back in the car, ready to visit the top of the world, as Grandad had put it.

John O'Groats was busy, which was to be expected, it being a famous location and a dry, sunny day. The drive in was quite flat with a sign greeting visitors to 'the end of the road.' We found a parking space, had a wander around the gift shops and queued up to have our photo taken beside the infamous sign.

'Eight hundred and seventy-four miles to Land's End,' I pointed out to Finn. 'That could be our next adventure, driving from here to there.'

'Our next adventure, eh? An annual road trip?'

The idea thrilled me. I shrugged. 'Why not?'

'Sounds awesome.'

He took hold of my hand as we strolled along the shoreline for a while. It felt comfortable, nice, normal, even. We could see the Isle of Stroma across the water.

'I'd like to go there,' said Finn, looking out. 'Hop around the Orkney islands.'

'Me too, I bet it's really peaceful.'

'A third trip then, we'll be travelling companions, having sex all over the British Isles.'

I laughed, the thought warming my insides. We walked on.

'There's something about the energy here, the vibe. I don't know...' He hesitated. 'It's just special. Sorry,' he shrugged. 'I'm probably talking nonsense.'

'No.' I shook my head. 'I totally get what you mean, there's a feeling of calm and positivity here. Maybe it's the vibrations of all the people who've travelled up from Lands End. They must have a massive sense of achievement.'

'And all the anticipation of the folks about to do it in reverse.'

'Exactly.'

We got veggie burgers and chips and found a picnic bench to sit and watch the world go by for a while. Then we drove to Dunnet Head, the most northerly point of the British mainland. I had previously thought it was John o' Groats, proving you learn something new every day. Another little walk, a few photos and we were on our way to the next hotel, just a few miles down the road.

'I'm really tired, do you mind if we just go to sleep?' I said, dumping my bag next to the bed.

Finn laughed. 'Of course not. That's not the deal you know; we don't have to have sex every night.'

'I know,' I said, although I didn't. I had kind of thought it might be... expected.

'Just every other night,' he said, winking and going into the bathroom.

I got changed, washed, and fell asleep as soon as my head hit the pillow. Or, rather, Finn's chest. I woke up around 3am and decided to wake him.

'I think we should make up for the hot sex we missed last night,' I said, climbing on top of him. He didn't protest.

It was past 9:50am when we woke, leaving us exactly ten minutes to check out. Hitting the road again, we were detouring slightly from the NC500 today. My Grandad had travelled to Tongue, a small town on the far north coast, then ventured south a little, to a village called Lairg. That was where he met Nora, and where some of my relatives still lived. I couldn't wait to get there.

Chapter Fifteen

Nora. 1973

It was Tom's idea to take the children on a Scottish holiday, including visiting John O'Groats. He'd gone there before with his friend, when they went on their road trip, but I'd never been. He said we should show them the top of the world, have a little holiday, and spend some quality time together. So, after a lovely week staying with my parents, we headed north for a few days.

It was easier, by then, travelling with the children. Frank was 11, and Moira 8. They were old enough to amuse themselves, although they did argue and bicker about sweets, about space in the car, and about the rules of certain games they were playing. It drove me slightly insane. Tom would laugh at them and tell them to behave. Always more patient than me, thank goodness.

We took a packed lunch that my mother had prepared and we set off through the highlands. I pointed out places I knew, while the children showed little interest, but Tom asked questions. He already knew the answers, but he just liked hearing me talk about my childhood.

A signpost had been erected since Tom had visited, and he insisted we have a family photo beside it. He told us the tale of visiting with his friend Mike, and we ate our sandwiches and wandered along the shoreline.

We stayed in a hotel that night and in the morning, took a ferry across to Orkney, where Frank declared we really were at the very top of the world. We walked, played games, and sat on the beach when the weather was good enough. It was wonderful.

I remember clearly watching Tom, paddling in the freezing cold sea with our children, and thinking how incredibly lucky I was. Thirty-two, and I had everything I could want.

I thought back to the days of uncertainty before I'd met him; I hadn't known if I wanted to get married, or have children, or where I'd end up. I'd felt like I was drifting, waiting for something interesting to happen, for life to begin.

And now, here I was, with my questions about the future answered. I was going to appreciate every moment. It felt good to be here, breathing Scottish air and watching this family, this magical thing Tom and I had created, having fun, and living a happy existence.

We stayed a few more days with my parents before we went home. Tom helped around the farm. The children ran wild with their cousins. I had good conversations with my parents, brother, and sister-in-law. Mal had taken on a lot of the work these days and had every intention of taking over the farm from Dad when he retired, which made me happy; the farm would stay in the family. I'd always have this place to return to, whenever I wanted.

On our last night, we had a big family meal, and laughed so much.

I was smiling all the way home, content with my lot and refuelled from my time in the Highlands.

I didn't know, then, that life was so very short.

A few months later, my father died. It was sudden; his heart just stopped. He was a healthy man, or so we'd thought. He didn't drink in excess, was slim, didn't smoke. He worked the fields until the day he dropped dead in our front yard. It made me face reality with a sharp shock. I returned home for a few weeks, to help with everything and to mourn with my mother and brother. Tom and the children came for the funeral.

'People always say how short life is,' my brother Mal said the night before I went home, 'but you never really believe it until someone you love is taken too soon.'

We talked about supporting Mum and the farm, about living life fully, making more time to see each other; all the things you say when you've had a shock like that. You make promises to yourself, and others, that you won't waste a moment of your precious life.

But then, life gets in the way, and you go back to being the way you were before.

The thing is, you never think it'll happen to you. I thought I would reach old age.

I thought Tom and I would grow old together.

I shouldn't have taken it for granted.

Chapter Sixteen

Marianne

Before I'd left for Scotland, I spent a day with my dad. He'd always been a wonderful man; kind and caring. I could remember him telling me about my grandmother Nora when I was a kid, but it'd been years since we'd spoken about her in any detail.

I took the journal to his house one Sunday, and Dad had a flick through, smiling at the photographs and mumbling 'ah, I didn't know that' a few times as he read little anecdotes and scribblings from his father, my Grandad Tom. My Grandmother Nora had put a few things in too, towards the end.

'I'm going to follow his journey,' I told Dad. 'I've quit my job and I've got money saved.'

'You quit your job?' Dad's eyes looked up for a moment, showing his concern, then back down to the journal. He was always very laid back and quietly confident that things would work out however they were meant to.

'Fresh start,' I explained, biting my lip. 'And it's definitely over with Ethan, too.'

Dad slowly closed the journal and let it rest on his lap. He looked at the floor for a moment, thinking. And then he looked up and said, 'he was never right for you, Love.'

Useful. Really useful.

'Well, why didn't you say something before I married him then?'

My mind flicked back for a moment. No, nothing. No hint. Dad had been supportive, and kind to Ethan. He'd walked me down the aisle proudly. I had no clue he didn't like my husband. None.

'It wasn't my place.'

'You're my father! If anyone had a right to an opinion, it was you!'

'Would it have made any difference?'

I thought about it for a moment. 'No,' I admitted. 'Probably not.'

'Well then, you would've just been annoyed with me. You had to figure it out for yourself.'

I sighed. 'Yes. I guess you're right.'

Don't you hate that, though? When others know you're making a mistake, and you have no idea until later?

'You could visit our relatives in Lairg,' he got up, 'I'll find the address for you, I don't have a phone number, but they always send me Christmas cards.'

'I had no idea.' I don't know why it hadn't occurred to me before, but my grandmother Nora's family hadn't really been talked of. 'So, what, I've got cousins?'

'Yes, and my Uncle Mal is still around I believe, so that's your great-uncle. His son Neil and daughter-in-law Maggie run what was my grandfather's farm. No sheep, anymore. They grow organic veg-etables, I believe.'

I'd never met any of them. 'Okay, so should I just show up, do you think? Or try to find a phone number, write a letter?'

'I don't see why you can't just show up. Uncle Mal was always very welcoming when I was a lad. We used to visit most summers when I was growing up.'

'Thanks, Dad.'

We made idle chit-chat about my sisters and their kids, and then I made to leave.

'So, you're off on quite the adventure then. Have a great time.'

'Thanks, Dad. I'm hoping it'll give me some space and time to figure out what I might do next. I'm excited, it'll be a soul-searching adventure.'

'Good for you, Love. Good for you. You've enough money?'

'Well, Ethan said he doesn't want any contribution towards the bills, so I have very little outgoings. Really, it's just my mobile phone bill, car insurance, food, hotels, that sort of thing. I've got some savings, so I'm going to use those. I suppose we'll sell the house when I get back, and I'll have to set myself up someplace new.'

'Good, well sounds like you've got everything in order. Keep in touch, Love.'

I kissed him goodbye and toddled off, back to my sister Jane's house. When I checked my bank balance the next day, he'd transferred me two thousand pounds. Bless him.

Mum, on the other hand, wasn't very supportive. She was a big fan of Ethan, and not such a big fan of Scotland. Or women travelling alone. Or me quitting my job. My sisters were behind me though, and since I'd arrived in Scotland, I'd posted regular photos online, and they'd been liking and commenting and keeping in touch.

I had a text from Tess, my younger sister, which I read out loud to Finn as we turned off the North Coast 500 route to head south on the road to Lairg. I'd booked us a cottage for a few nights, not far from my relatives. I was anxious about dropping in unannounced, yet excited to see the farm my grandmother Nora grew up on.

'This is from Tess,' I told Finn. 'My younger sister: "OMG, who is this guy you've met? He is very handsome indeed!"'

I laughed and tucked my phone away.

'You posted photos of us together on your social media?' Finn asked, staring ahead at the road.

'Oops, sorry, would you rather I didn't?'

'Doesn't bother me. Might bother Ethan, that's all.'

'I doubt he's following me,' I told him. 'I'm sure he would have unfollowed me a while ago. I don't care what he thinks anyway, he specifically said many months ago that we should feel free to see other people.'

'Fair enough,' Finn said, turning up the music. I'd made a special road trip playlist and we both sang along to the eclectic mix, enjoying the constantly changing beautiful views. We stopped regularly to take photos as the landscape changed. We saw thousands of trees, hills, mountains, sheep and gorgeous highland cows (Finn called them *heeland coos*, which I much preferred).

'This is the best road ever,' Finn said as we saw yet another glorious view. I was driving. 'I'm so glad we detoured from the NC500; we'd have missed this whole area. Thank you.'

'I'll pass the gratitude to Grandad Tom. He promised every shade of green, and Scotland has delivered.'

We found our rental cottage, dumped our stuff, and headed out to the family farm, me a bundle of nerves, Finn extremely curious to meet my Scottish relatives. I was curious too, but I felt weird about just turning up. I didn't have a phone number though so there was little choice.

We pulled up in a stone driveway, and I recognised the big white house from an old photo of my grandparents. I pulled it out of the journal and held it, along with a couple of other photos of my grandmother and the one of Nana Bea, too. Finn hung back a few steps as I knocked on the blue front door.

It took a few minutes, but a friendly face soon answered, about my grandad's age.

'Malcolm?' I asked.

'Yes? Can I help you?' he squinted, as if he recognised me.

'I'm Marianne,' I said. 'Your great niece. Nora's granddaughter?'

'Oh, my word!' He threw his arms around me. I hugged him awkwardly, then relaxed in his warm embrace. He smelled like Grandad, a hint of talc and Old Spice aftershave. I gestured towards my handsome companion. 'This is my friend, Finn.'

'Well, ye both of you had better come in.'

I had been expecting some sort of time capsule, to be transported back to 1960, but of course things had changed since Nora and Tom met. Everything was very minimal inside, with white walls, oak furniture, and a huge, beautiful bouquet of wildflowers on the dining table.

Mal made us tea, which we took through to a large sitting room. I showed him the photos, and he found an old box and showed me more. I felt emotional, seeing childhood photos of Nora, and he offered for me to take some copies with my phone, to share with my dad and sisters.

'Oh hello, Bruno,' Mal held out his hand to a gorgeous tabby cat who strolled in. Bruno ignored Mal and came straight over to me. I leaned down to give him a big fuss.

'Oh, you're beautiful,' I told him as he purred. I glanced up at Finn, who was smiling at me.

'She loves cats,' he told Mal.

'Just like her Nana Nora,' Mal said, grinning. 'You're like her in many ways, it's uncanny.' I beamed with pride, realising that any connection to the grandmother I'd never met was special to me.

After an hour or so, Mal's son, Neil, arrived home with his wife Maggie. They were just as welcoming. They had children, all grown and living in Edinburgh and Glasgow. We went outside and they showed us the farm. The house was on a hill, and in the valley below you could see the fields where they grew peas, broad beans and other vegetables.

'All organic,' Mal told me proudly. 'When Neil told me he had big changes for the farm, I wasn't impressed if I'm honest, but he's done so well, kept us going, and his daughter Corina wants to take it to the next level, too. I'm amazed we've kept it in the family.'

'That's wonderful,' I said, watching him well up. 'I'm so glad. And so pleased I get to meet you all, finally.'

'I wish... I wish I'd visited Nora. When she moved south, I was always so busy with the farm, and then our father died, and I had even more to do. I should have gone down.'

'I'm sure she understood,' I told him. 'My dad says they visited you most summers?'

'Yes,' Mal smiled at the memories. 'Until Nora was gone. Then I think Tom, your grandad, well, he found it too hard to come back here.'

'We should organise a big family reunion,' I told him, sure that both Dad and Grandad would be up for it if we all visited together.

'That'd be wonderful,' Mal said, his eyes misty. He put his arm around me. 'Nora's granddaughter, here to visit us. Well, I never.'

Maggie insisted we stay for dinner and didn't even flinch when I said I didn't eat meat. She made a delicious pasta dish with peas, onions and olive oil and served it with homemade bread and local cider.

'She looks like my sister so much,' Mal said to Neil, nudging him with his elbow. 'She's a Lindsay, for sure.'

I felt myself sit a little taller. I'd always felt desperate to know more about my grandmother, so sad not to have met her. For her brother to welcome me so warmly, to say I looked like her, that I was one of them... it re-confirmed my belief that, despite my English accent and

Leicestershire upbringing, my Scottish roots were the reason I'd been called to come here for so long. The reason I felt tied to this land.

We had a wonderful evening, chatting about this and that, sharing both memories of the past and details of our present lives. Finn was friendly, funny, and fit right in. Everyone seemed to like him and made him as welcome as me.

'This has been wonderful,' I told them, giving hugs goodbye. 'Thank you so much for the warm welcome and now I've got your number, we can keep in touch.'

'You make sure to do that,' Neil said, hugging me tight. 'And say hello to that cousin of mine, tell him to get himself up here. Your dad and I used to play in the summer holidays when they came to visit. I've a lot of fond memories.'

'I will, thank you.'

'Now, you keep in touch young Marianne, you hear?' Mal said, giving me a long, hard hug. 'You really do remind me a lot of my sister,' he said, pulling away and looking at my face.

'Thank you, that means a lot.'

'Didn't you have a husband?' he whispered. 'Ewan or Owen or something? Your aunt Moira writes to me sometimes.'

'Ethan, yes that didn't work out.'

'Well, you keep hold of this one,' he said, gesturing to Finn, who was standing by the car. 'I like him. He's a keeper.'

'Maybe so,' I said, and promised one more time to keep in touch.

'Haste ye back!' he called, as I waved through the open car window.

It was a mild evening, so Finn and I sat outside our rental cottage for a while in the small garden. We were on the side of a large hill, with a view down into the valley. The view was stunning.

'So, I'm a keeper, eh?' Finn said, taking a sip of hot tea. He must have heard Mal talking to me before we left.

'Don't worry, I'm not getting any ideas of keeping you,' I said, a little too sharply, without looking at him.

The only thing I was keeping: my feelings in check. Well, mostly. Some of the time.

'We'll see,' he said, drinking some more tea. What did that mean?

'I can't believe how light it still is,' I said, changing the subject swiftly.

It was almost midnight, and the sky was just a dusky blue, still very light with a white glow on the horizon.

'In midsummer it doesn't get dark in the highlands,' Finn stood, taking his tea to the garden fence. He leaned against it, looking out at the view. I went to join him.

'It's beautiful, isn't it?' I said, taking in the eerie light. It was almost midnight, but still light. I didn't think anything could pull me away from this beautiful view.

'Just like you,' he said, turning towards me. 'Race you to the bedroom?'

Of course, Finn could pull me away from the view. I turned and sprinted for the house. I'm human, after all. A woman has needs. Needs Finn knew exactly how to fill.

I woke up at 4am and couldn't breathe, it was as if some invisible force was sucking air from my lungs while my heart rate climbed. I stared at the ceiling, trying to calm myself but it felt like the room was spinning, wild and out of control. I hadn't had a panic attack in so long, I wondered for a moment if I could actually be having a heart attack.

I managed to sit up, then slipped out of the bed as quietly as I could. I crept slowly down the stairs in my pyjamas, opened the front door of the cottage, stepped out into the cool air, and gasped for breath.

My heart was beating wildly and for a moment I thought I was going to die. I looked out at the stunning view; the sun had risen again and was glinting on Loch Shin in the distance. *Not a bad place to die*, I thought to myself as I lowered myself down onto the grass on all fours.

'Marianne, are you okay?' Finn's voice came from behind me. I didn't want him to see, I wanted him to be sound asleep and blissfully unaware that I wasn't the fun, adventurous girl he thought, but a complete wreck.

I managed to nod.

'What's wrong?' he asked, coming to crouch in front of me. I sank back on my bottom and crossed my legs.

'I just...' I couldn't speak.

'Panic attack?' he asked, taking my hands. How did he know?

I stared at his eyes, as mine filled up with tears.

'You're okay, just breathe,' he said calmly. 'You're doing great.'

I kept focusing on his eyes, and as if by magic, after a few minutes I felt my body release the tension and my breathing returned to normal.

And then, as if this wasn't embarrassing enough, I burst into tears.

He held me, as I sobbed into his chest and the damp grass soaked my pyjamas.

'It's okay,' he said, gently rubbing my back. But it wasn't okay. Nothing was okay. This trip, it was wonderful. I felt at peace; calm and content. I had started to like myself more. I liked the Marianne who was around Finn. But it was coming to an end soon, and I had no idea what would happen next, where I'd go or what I'd do. I was so scared of returning to that dark, depressed state I'd been in before.

Eventually, my tears stopped, and he just held me there for a while.

'Do you want to talk about it?' he asked.

'Not really.'

'That's fine.'

We were silent for a few moments, and then I thought: what do I have to lose? Maybe it'll help.

'Before this trip… I was in a bad place for a while. Depression and anxiety. I got better, I had some therapy and things improved. I suppose I'm scared of sinking back again when this is all over.'

'I get that. But you've grown a lot by the sounds of it? You had your therapy. And you're doing this trip. You've been connecting to your spiritual side. You've been thinking about what you want. All that will help.'

'Yes,' I whispered, my head still on his chest, his arms wrapped around me. I'd somehow gone from feeling terrified to extremely safe and I didn't want to move.

'And if not, you got through it before, you'll get through it again.'

'Thank you, Finn.' A few more tears fell.

'Do you think… sorry it's none of my business.'

'No, it's okay. What?'

'Do you think your mental health contributed to your breakup with Ethan?'

'It was a catalyst, for sure. He didn't get it. Wanted me to just get a grip and cheer up.'

'Sometimes, I think, you have to have experienced mental health challenges for yourself, to fully understand what someone else is going through.'

'Sounds like you know what you're talking about.' I said, sitting back to look at him. I was damp and cold, but not ready to get up yet.

'Well, I lost my sister. I loved my job in the fire service, but I saw a lot of people on their very worst day, saw people lose loved ones. I held that kid that died, her name was Rosie. I held Rosie in my arms and saw her take her last breath. It took a while to get over that.'

'Of course it did. Your sister… Do you think about Clara a lot?'

'Every day. Sometimes it's just a nice memory. Other times it's about her death. The therapy helped but, I don't know, sometimes I just can't get her face out of my head. Those last few seconds when she was begging me to agree to raise her baby girl.'

He choked on the last few words, swallowing hard. My eyes filled with tears again.

'And the child. Rosie. That must've... it's just horrendous, Finn.'

He took a deep breath. 'It's part of the job, but yes. That messed with me for a long while. It's been tough.'

'Yet you seem so grounded,' I said, smiling and taking a deep breath.

'That's taken a lot of work, trust me.' He smiled back. 'And to be honest, being around you. Well, it's helped. A lot. Not sure what this trip would have been like without you.'

'Same here.'

We smiled at each other, but I just felt sad. This had no future.

'Now,' he said, squeezing me. 'I think we'd better get you in some warm clothes.'

He stood up, and held out his hands, which I took, and he pulled me up.

'You okay now?' he asked, and I nodded.

'Thank you, Finn.'

'Anytime,' he said, taking me by the hand into the cottage.

It wouldn't be 'any time' though, would it? Our time together was limited, and I was beginning to realise that might be even more heart-breaking than leaving my marriage.

He ran a hot bath for me and put some laundry on while I was in there. We waited for the tumble drier to finish, and then spent the day walking locally, taking it easy, a nice respite from all the driving.

The next morning, we were back on the road.

Chapter Seventeen

Marianne

Not far from the cottage, and my relatives' farm, are the Falls of Shin. We decided to go see them before we left the area. Maggie insisted it'd be worth it to see the salmon leaping upstream. There's a platform, above some falls, and we stared for a while, watching, waiting... waiting... and then exclaiming and pointing whenever we saw a salmon try to leap, often unsuccessfully. I'd give a little 'yay' when I finally saw one make it.

'You're sweet,' Finn said. 'Rooting for them like that.'

'They have to fulfil their destiny,' I told him. 'The salmon swim upstream to spawn.'

'What folks do to have babies, eh.' He laughed.

'Most seem to think it's worthwhile,' I chuckled. I glanced at him, and again he was looking thoughtful, like he had when I'd mentioned I didn't want babies before.

It took about an hour to drive back north to Tongue and pick up the North Coast 500 route again. Passing back along the road we'd travelled yesterday, I felt different. Finn had seen a dark part of me, a part I'd been hoping had disappeared, or was at least hiding for the long-term. I'd visited my grandmother's childhood home and met relatives I'd never seen before. How could so much have happened in such a short space of time? I'd felt so at home in this area, I knew I'd be back. I'd have to find a job – although I had no clue what work would be available in remote highland areas. I had to find out and see if I could make it work. I could see myself living near Mal and this part of my family. I could see myself walking the land, spending time with these lovely people, making a home here. For the first time since I'd decided to leave Ethan, I felt like a plan might be forming. My mind was processing, and I was quiet as I drove.

Finn put on some relaxing music, making conversation about the scenery, pointing out different views. I agreed with all his enthusiastic remarks. I loved the trees and hills and vistas, but I remained fairly quiet.

'You okay?' he asked as we reached Tongue and I took the turning back onto the NC500.

'Sure, I am,' I said, smiling. 'Tongue. Who came up with these place names, eh?'

'Pull over at this spot up ahead,' he said. 'It's my turn to drive.'

I pulled in, got out, and he squeezed my hand as we passed at the rear of the car. I slid into the passenger seat and on we went, making light conversation but mostly in silence, snacking on grapes and slowing down now and then to take in the landscape.

The next part of the trip was travelling along the north coast to-wards Durness. The road took us past sea views, hills, mountains, trees, and lots of beautiful heather. Eventually it led us to the shores of Loch Eriboll. The weather wasn't as good, but still dry and the grey clouds even added a moody atmosphere.

Without speaking, Finn pulled up in a parking space, suggested we eat our lunch, grabbed his bag and hopped out. He laid out a blanket on a patch of grass and I sat beside him.

It was chilly, and I did up my coat. I didn't mind being cold, though. The view was spectacular; rolling hills and mountains on the horizon.

The loch lay in front of us; grey blue with the clouds' reflection moving across the water.

I took a deep breath, inhaling the fresh, salty air.

'I love it here,' I said quietly.

'Me too.' Finn smiled at me. 'You don't have to talk about it,' he said, passing me a bottle of water. 'But you've been a little quiet today, I hope you're alright.'

'I'm okay, I'm sorry if I've been a little distant.'

'It's fine, I think we're at that stage where the occasional silence is comfortable.'

'Did you have panic attacks?' I asked suddenly, surprising myself. Perhaps knowing what was going on in his life would help me forget about my own. 'You seemed to know what one felt like, that's all.'

He took a deep breath.

'I'm sorry, I'm being nosey.'

'No, it's okay,' he said. 'It's just that, other than therapy, I've not talked about it much.'

'Only share if you want to.'

'Rosie, the girl who died as I held her, well, she was the same age as Iona. And I used to have a lot of nightmares. But it wasn't Rosie, it was Iona. My precious girl, dead in my arms.' He was staring straight ahead, his face hard. 'I'd wake up and feel like I was dying.' He shrugged. 'Couldn't breathe, heart racing. Well, you know how it feels. The first time, I didn't know what was going on, and it scared the crap out of me. But I kind of got used to it. And after a while, they eased up.'

'Oh Finn. I can't even imagine what those dreams felt like.'

It made my issues feel trivial in comparison to what he'd been through.

'The nightmares have stopped.' He picked a piece of grass and fiddled with it, then looked out at the horizon. 'Things are better now.'

'You're a hero,' I said, imagining him running into a burning building to save a child, only to carry out a lifeless body. My eyes misted up.

'No,' he said modestly. 'I just did my job.'

'So, you took a leave of absence?'

'After my leg healed, I went back. But I kept having panic attacks.'

'You needed a break.'

'One time, on the job, we were helping this guy out; he'd got stuck in a tree and couldn't get down. It wasn't as serious as a fire, but I froze. I had to sit down and take deep breaths.'

'That must have been hard, in front of your colleagues.'

'Yep. I mean, they were all great. But I requested a few months off, unpaid of course. And then decided I didn't want to go back.'

'That's understandable.'

'I was Deputy Chief. My Chief has been really understanding, especially around my feelings with Iona and the risks of the job. She suggested I stay with the service but take a different role. Training recruits maybe.'

'How do you feel about that?'

He nodded. 'Yeah, I can see myself doing something like that, but I also feel like I might need a clean break. I love being outdoors and I've been talking to a pal of mine who's a ranger. He does conservation work, like monitoring wild bird populations, clearing trails and tracking visitor numbers. All sorts. I'd get to be outdoors, in nature and after the intensity of my last job... well, it'd be peaceful.'

'That's amazing. I can absolutely see you doing that.'

'I guess I want something that's good for my mental health, and less shift work so I can be there for Iona.'

I thought about how much he'd talked about the outdoors, how he seemed to love getting out walking with Iona. And what better place to do it, than the wilderness of Britain's largest national park? 'You'd be great at it.'

He smiled, dropped the blade of grass, and picked up his sandwich. 'Thanks. You know, you're very easy to talk to.'

'Likewise.' It was so easy, it scared me a little.

I took a bite of an apple, realising it'd be my turn next.

'So, what about you?' he asked gently. 'Any catalyst moment that started the panic attacks?'

'To be honest, nothing. I can't claim a horrific incident happened or even put it down to anything particular.'

'That's okay, though. It doesn't make it any less valid.'

'I was depressed, and it came on slowly. I didn't really like my job and felt unfulfilled in general. I'd fallen out of love with Ethan but wasn't able to admit it yet. I stopped having any fun. I drifted away from my friends and family. I didn't take care of myself. It just got worse and worse, until I was in a pit of despair.'

I'd been looking out at the loch, so I glanced at Finn. He was watching me. 'I wish I'd known you then,' he said gently. 'I wish I could've helped you.'

I felt so overcome with feeling for him that I had to swallow to stop from crying. I took a deep breath and continued.

'It got to the point where even going outside was pushing my comfort zone. Challenging myself in any way made me extremely anxious. It was a vicious circle really because I stayed at home, eating junk, and staring into space all day. That meant I also didn't have any pleasure or joy, or feel very happy. And then I put on weight and felt crap about myself, and embarrassed.'

He nodded encouragingly.

'I don't know why I was depressed, or so anxious. I just was. And I couldn't see a way to dig myself out of the pit I'd fallen into.'

'And yet you did, you're here now, doing this. You should be proud of yourself.'

I hadn't thought of it like that. I'd come a long way; he was right. To think that the depressed version of me could barely get off the sofa, and yet here I was, travelling around Scotland with a random guy I'd met only a few weeks ago. It made me sit a little taller.

'My therapist helped me a lot,' I told him. 'She gave me some mindfulness techniques. She helped me to slowly start changing my behaviour and getting on with living, instead of wallowing.'

'It's hard to force yourself to get help, and harder still to put the advice into action. Well done you. When did you know you were better?'

I gulped. 'I guess I'm still getting better.'

'Sure,' he said, opening some crisps and offering me one. 'But you're doing better than you were, right?'

'Oh yes of course,' I smiled. 'Miles better. I guess I should give myself some credit for how far I've come.'

'Definitely. It's not easy digging yourself out.'

'I think the moment things turned around, was when I admitted I didn't want to be with Ethan anymore. It was like a weight had been lifted. He didn't mean to, but he held me back. He wanted a safe life, didn't like bold decisions or spontaneity. If I said I wanted a new job, he'd remind me that I had good benefits and was secure where I was. When I said I wanted to go to Scotland, he advised that the Canary Islands would be warmer.'

'Well, that's a fair point,' Finn said, winking at me. A warm ache pooled between my legs, as it always did when he looked at me intently. I felt the lust surge through, just as it did every day of the trip. We'd had passionate, mind-blowing sex almost every day and I wasn't sure how I'd cope without it when the trip was done. Was there such a thing as sexy fling withdrawal? I'd better look it up, to be prepared.

'I prefer it here,' I said, as I watched a flock of birds soaring above us. 'I like adventure, and mountains and alpine trees and lochs, way more than palm trees, cocktails and sunbeds.'

'Well, for my benefit, I'm glad.'

My phone started to ring. 'Oh,' I said, showing Finn that it was Ethan. 'His ears must've been burning.'

'Take it,' Finn said, rummaging around for more picnic food.

'I won't be long,' I said, standing up and walking a little distance away.

'Ethan?'

'Marianne, hi.'

I wanted to say *why are you calling me*, but decided to keep it friendly. None of this was his fault, certainly no more than mine.

'How are you?'

'I'm okay. Are you enjoying your time in Scotland?'

'Yes. It's beautiful.' What did he want, and how fast could I get off the phone?

'Honestly, I'm jealous,' he said, and I nearly burst out laughing.

'No, you're not,' I said sharply. 'You never wanted to come here.'

'I don't mean where you are. You met someone new, I see. Didn't take you long.'

So, he'd been snooping online, after all. Perhaps I shouldn't have posted any photos with Finn.

'He's just a friend.'

'You look happy, Marianne.'

'I guess I am.' Panic-attack yesterday aside, I meant it. I glanced back at Finn, who was looking down at his phone, typing a text.

'So, if he's just a friend. I was thinking perhaps I could come up there. Where are you now?'

What? *What?!*

'Why would you do that, Ethan?'

'I miss you.'

I sighed. 'Ethan, you're just lonely.'

'But it used to be good. What if we had couples counselling? Talked about our issues? Surely, we don't just give up, just like that?'

'I don't think marriage counselling would help.' I glanced again at Finn, on the blanket. He was watching me, but quickly looked away. I wondered if he could hear what I was saying.

'Will you at least think about it?'

'Ethan,' I said, taking a deep breath and only realising what I wanted as the words came out of my mouth: 'We need to get a divorce.'

His voice was calm, but he sighed.

'Marianne, come on. You're going to throw away everything we had?'

'We talked about this. We're not in love. You just miss being a couple.'

'Do you love this guy?'

'What?'

'The guy you're travelling with.'

So, this was what it was about; he didn't miss me. He was just jealous. Of Finn, but perhaps also of me, for being the first one to move on.

I looked back at Finn. He was staring out at the view. 'Of course I don't love him, we're just friends.'

'Okay. Have you had sex with him?'

'That's none of your business, we are separated. Besides, you're the one who said we should see other people.'

'I thought you were going on your own, you could've told me you'd met someone.'

'I met him here, for the record.'

'Right,' he sighed. 'Well, I hope you're enjoying yourself.'

'I'm sorry Ethan, I'm so sad that we got to this point. But we're not in love anymore and haven't been for a long time. We both need to move on. Sell the house, get a divorce. A fresh start. It's for the best.'

He was silent for a moment, then ended the call.

I took a breath, put the phone in my pocket and stood still for a moment. I then went back to Finn, smiled, and sat back down to resume my lunch.

'Everything okay?'

'Could you hear?'

'Afraid so.'

'I think, it's just...' I couldn't articulate it.

'You don't have to explain to me.'

'No, I want to. I think it'd help.'

'Take your time.'

'I think meeting you made me realise what he and I were missing all along.'

I didn't expect those words to come out, but I knew immediately they were true. He stared at me for what felt like a long moment, then swallowed.

'How do you mean?'

I shook my head. Was I implying I had stronger feelings for Finn than I ever had for Ethan? Why was I saying these words out loud? We had no future. I could ruin this trip. This fun, sexy, adventurous holiday could be over in a flash.

'Ethan and I weren't friends,' I said, slowly, speaking the truth but also holding a lot back. 'You and I, yes the sex is amazing but also-'

'Best I've ever had,' he interrupted, smiling.

'*Really*?' I couldn't believe that – he was a gorgeous fireman, he'd probably had all sorts of beautiful women throwing themselves at him.

'Really.'

Wow, that made me feel all kinds of wonderful.

'With you,' I said, trying to explain without sounding too romantic, 'it's like being with a best friend. I can talk to you about anything. We have a similar outlook on life, similar values.'

'We do,' he said, looking away into the distance. 'On most things.'

'Ethan and I, we were good together at the beginning but honestly, it got boring. We didn't have much to talk about, whereas you and I can talk non-stop. And, we didn't share the same outlook, or vision for the future.'

'Okay, so what is your vision for the future?'

'Ha, good question! Right now, it's kind of vague. I do know I want to live somewhere like this, somewhere green and beautiful. I want to do a job that somehow helps others. And I want a cat.'

He laughed. 'Sounds like it's achievable.'

I smiled, nodding my head. 'It does. So, what about you,' I asked, nervous about the answer but unsure why. 'Have you had many relationships?'

He looked away. 'No, I mean, nothing serious. It's complicated with Iona, I wouldn't let just anyone in, you know? That person would have to take Iona, too, which is a lot to ask of any woman.'

'I get that,' I nodded. 'But the right person will come along, and she'll embrace you both.'

The thought of him falling in love with someone made me want to vomit my lunch back up.

'It'd also just feel weird, you know. Like I'm trying to replace my sister, find Iona a new mother. I already feel bad that she calls me Dad. John was supposed to have that role.'

'I think Clara and John would want you to be happy, for Iona to have as many people as possible to love her.'

Finn glanced at me, glassy eyed, then flicked his eyes away again quickly. 'I'd never thought of it like that before.'

'It must be a contradiction of feelings.'

He nodded. 'Yes, it is. Losing my sister was the worst thing that's ever happened to me. But adopting Iona has been the best. How those two things can go hand-in-hand is just...'

He sighed.

'A conflict of thoughts and emotion,' I tried to find the words for him.

'Exactly. Thank you, I don't think anyone has ever understood before. Probably because I've not really talked to many people about it.'

I squeezed his hand. 'Well, this has been quite the deep and meaningful pitstop.'

He smiled. 'It has.'

Finn wanted to call Iona, and wandered off for a little while, leaving me to think about everything I'd said, and Ethan's call.

If I'd been here alone, would I have said yes to Ethan – told me to come join me? Would I have been so desperately lonely that I'd have taken him back, tried marriage counselling, fallen back into my old life? Possibly.

I watched Finn, smiling and talking animatedly to the daughter he so willingly adopted. I felt my heart swell with – what? Lust? Warmth? Admiration? All of those things.

There was no way I'd ever consider being with Ethan again, now I knew there was more. I already felt closer, more connected, more grounded, more everything with Finn than I ever had with Ethan. It defied logic, but in this short space of time, I'd found real *emotional intimacy*. I realised with a bolt of awareness that was exactly what Ethan and I had lacked all along.

Sure, I had once loved Ethan enough to marry him. The younger, more ignorant, less self-aware me had thought what we had was special. And it was, in its own way, at the time.

But Finn... Being with Finn was a whole new level of intimacy and connection. It was more than chemistry. It was soul-deep, knowing to my core that I could spend forever with him, and it wouldn't be enough.

As these thoughts washed over me, I was rigid, watching him meander about as he spoke to Iona. I was terrified of how strongly I felt. These feelings didn't change the fact that I didn't want children, and the reaction he'd had when I mentioned that. Not to mention he already had one. He also had a very different life, very far from everything I knew. It couldn't possibly work and he didn't want a relationship. He'd made it clear he only wanted to be friends. With benefits. But still only friends.

I packed up the blanket and our stuff, put it in the car, then leaned against it as I watched him walking back towards me.

I was falling in love with Finn. It was petrifying, and painfully impossible.

I just had to enjoy the rest of our trip. Say goodbye. And then maybe, just maybe, I'd meet someone else I could feel like this about one day. At least now I knew what I was looking for.

Or maybe, I'd get a houseful of cats and live out my days devoted to them, telling them the stories of the handsome man who'd taken me on a Scottish adventure.

Back in the car, on our way to Durness, I forced myself to be more chatty and 'normal' this time. Despite my painful, already broken heart, coping with the fact I couldn't have a future with the man I was crazy about.

I was determined to enjoy the next few days, to soak in every moment of pure blissful time with Finn and commit as much of it to memory as I could.

I happily informed him that the beaches up ahead had been voted some of the best in the world. This led to a conversation about the best beaches we'd ever visited (Myrtos Beach in Kefalonia, for me. For him, Carmel by the Sea in California).

'I went on a road trip with an ex-girlfriend, back in my early 20's,' he told me. 'It's epic.'

'I'm putting that on my bucket list,' I said, wistfully. 'I want to do loads of road trips after this one.'

'Maybe we can be road trip buddies. It could be an annual thing,' he said, not looking away from the road.

'I love that idea.' Seeing him once a year was better than never. But then again, wouldn't it just lead to a never-ending cycle of heartache? I put that thought away with the ever-growing list of things to think about later.

The views were wonderful, pure wilderness on both sides of the road. We saw a magnificent red stag, and eagles soaring above. And then we found ourselves at Ceannabeinne Beach, a pure slice of heaven. Grandad Tom had photos in his journal, but the grainy, black and white pictures didn't do this place any justice.

We pulled up in the car park, got out, walked a little way, then stood on the grass, taking it all in. I couldn't help myself; I slipped my hand into Finn's, and he squeezed it.

The landscape was lush, vivid green grass along the rocky cliffs. The untouched beach looked like something out of the Caribbean, with pale golden-white sand, craggy rocks and clear, azure water. The sun had come out just a little, lighting the whole scene up.

There wasn't anyone else around.

'Okay, this is the best beach I've ever seen,' I said. I mean, Greece is wonderful, but to see this tropical-looking scene along the grassy cliffs of my beloved Scotland... I couldn't wish to be anywhere else.

'Ditto,' said Finn, leading me by the hand over the grass, down the (not too steep) cliff and onto the sand. We walked right up to the clear water and put our hands in – it was freezing of course – and then walked along the shoreline. After a while we pulled out the blanket from Finn's bag and sat on it. I swirled my hands around in the sand.

'I can't believe we're still in Scotland,' Finn said, taking my hand again. I liked the steady support it offered, the heat of him, the closeness.

'Me either.'

'I also can't believe I've not been up here before.'

I asked him where he grew up, and he told me in Stirling.

'My sister moved to Aviemore after university. She worked as a nurse there. I visited and loved the whole area so decided I'd move up as well. Just as well, really, given what happened.'

'I don't blame you for moving there, I loved the Cairngorms.'

He looked thoughtful. 'Do you think you'd consider living there?'

'I think I need to figure out what job I might do first,' I admitted. 'Before I can figure out where to live.'

'Have you had any light bulb moments on that?'

I'd been churning some ideas for a few days, and it felt like it was time to talk them through.

'I want to help people,' I said, knowing as I said it, it was something I absolutely felt called to do. It was bigger than a 'want'.

'In my meditation, they said I was a Lightworker, and I looked it up. Teachers, life coaches, nurses and so on.'

'And?'

'I think I might want to do something to help people with their mental wellbeing. Teach meditation and mindfulness. Before my depression and all the weight gain, I was good at yoga, maybe I could become a teacher even. And maybe one day even offer services like Trina and offer spiritual coaching or mentoring. Or I could run a shop like Luna's. I feel called into this spiritual space and I've no idea yet what that'll look like.'

'That's amazing, so you'd open your own business?'

'Yes,' I said, feeling terrified and excited at the same time. 'I suppose I'll need an interim job to start with, to cover my rent or whatever while I do some training and get set up. I thought I'd create multiple streams of income. But I've no idea *where* this will all take place.'

'I find it hard to imagine you anywhere but Scotland,' he said, smiling.

'I suppose I could offer mindfulness and spiritual appointments online, so it might not matter where I live. Look at me, acting like I know what I'm talking about.'

'I'm so inspired,' Finn said, kissing me on the cheek. 'You're so brave.'

'Me? Brave? Ha! Did you not witness my panic attack?'

'Yes, brave! It took courage to walk away from the safety of your marriage, your job, your home. To come on this trip. To agree to travel with a stranger. To come up with an idea for a new business, a whole new life for yourself.'

'Well, yes when you list it like that, I suppose so. It all sounds quite scary.'

'Sorry, not trying to induce another panic attack,' he said, nudging me playfully. 'I just really admire you, and you ought to have higher self-esteem.'

'Well, I admire you. Adopting Iona. Being a firefighter. Recognising when you needed a break, that took courage too.'

He smiled and lay back on the blanket. I relaxed back too, staring up at the sky. I shivered.

'Cold?'

'Yup.'

'Do you want to go? We're not far from the next hotel.'

'Nope. I'd rather be cold, outdoors, here in this moment, with this beautiful sand and the sound of the sea, than inside a hotel.'

'Me too. I think this might be one of my Thin Places.'

'Thin place?' I'd never heard of that before.

'It's a place where you feel connected to... something bigger than you. The universe, God, a higher power, whatever you believe in. A place where it feels like the gap between heaven and Earth is thin. I'm not religious, just spiritual, but I've heard the term, and I've always thought it sounded wonderful. I think this might be it, my thin place.'

'Wow, me too,' I said, knowing exactly what he meant, how he felt. The whole of Scotland felt like my Happy Place but this particular beach; this made my soul soar.

My fingers found his hand again. I turned my head to his, and he turned his back to me. We kissed.

'This might be the most awesome friendship I've ever had,' he said, grinning.

I nodded. 'Same here,' I said, taking in those lovely, hazel eyes.

The whoosh of pure joyful feelings, the bliss, the intensity of what I felt for him in that moment was almost too much. I felt the urge to tell him how I felt, to ignore the fear, the complication that I didn't want to have a baby when he clearly did, the fact he lived far from everything I knew, that he had a niece-come-adopted-daughter and I didn't want that responsibility, at all... All those issues faded into the background as I stared at him, and he stared right back.

Then I shivered again, and he insisted we head off because it was getting late.

As we drove to our hotel in the village of Durness, he made idle chit-chat about Iona. All I could think was: *Phew! Thank goodness I didn't tell him how I feel!* Putting aside that he wanted a baby, I wasn't cut out for his life; I didn't want children and he already had one.

I was going to enjoy this friendship, this holiday fling or whatever you want to call it, then I was going to move on and create my brand-new life.

Chapter Eighteen

Nora. Mid-1970's

When my babies were toddlers, I remember my mother-in-law Esther telling me that this was the worst period of parenthood. Teaching them boundaries, that 'no' means 'no'. Dealing with tantrums. Helping Frank and Moira to understand that the world did not revolve around them.

She was wrong.

My toddlers were a breeze compared to how they were as teenagers.

Everyone expects toddlers to have tantrums; maybe they're tired, hungry, ill, or even testing their boundaries. Teenagers, well for me, they were a complete mystery.

How my darling, beautiful, kind, and considerate pair could become so difficult so quickly, was beyond me.

Frank wasn't quite so bad as Moira. He was aloof, and didn't say much. He wanted to go out with his friends as often as possible and got in trouble a few times for fighting. Sometimes he missed the last bus home and didn't turn up for dinner. Tom would have to drive to the local town to find him. Frank was closed off, and difficult, but I could cope with that.

Moira, it seemed, changed around midnight of her 13th birthday. Before that, she'd been interested in ponies, flowers, dolls, and make-believe.

During her early teen years, she was irritable, rude, and sometimes just plain cruel. She didn't try hard in school. She took no interest or pleasure in anything we wanted to do as a family. We'd argue all the time. Even Tom, with his calm friendly approach, couldn't get her to see sense. Even though she adored her father, she was rude to him too.

Some days I thought I'd lost the version of my daughter I knew, forever. I loved her, beyond anything, but I didn't like her very much.

She dropped out of school at the age of 15 and got a job working at Tom's place. By this point, he'd had an offer from a large corporation to buy the shoe factory. It was more money than we'd ever imagined, and he was going through the fine print. He'd stay on and run the place, so he'd still have a job. He talked about retiring early and getting some part-time work.

In the meantime, Moira went to work for him. Not that she enjoyed it. We asked her to pay a little board money, and she practically threw it at me each time it was due. If I asked her to help around the home, she glared like I was the worst mother in the world, which I felt most days.

'I don't know what I've done to deserve this,' I said to her one day.

She muttered something about me having no clue what it was like to be her and stomped off to her bedroom.

Tom was wonderfully patient, as always. Frank was kinder, and helped around the house. As he moved through the years, his interest in buildings grew, and he started talking about becoming an architect. He'd show me books he got from the library, talked about designs and showed me his sketches.

Meanwhile, Moira grew more and more unpleasant.

Some nights, Tom and I went out just to get away from the negative energy she was emitting day-in, day-out.

Then she met her first proper boyfriend, Ricky. And things got worse. Very quickly, Ricky was the be-all and end-all. In her mind, her family ceased to exist. I'd try to get her to talk, to share, to open up the way I'd done with my own mother when I was falling in love with Tom. I was lucky if she gave me more than a few minutes of her attention.

It started to affect me, it made me feel sad and tired.

'Do you ever wish we hadn't had children?' I asked Tom one day.

He looked at me in astonishment.

'She'll grow out of it,' he said. 'And no, of course not. How can you ask me that?'

'I never thought I'd have children,' I said. 'Before I met you.'

'Really?' he put down the newspaper he was reading. 'But you're a wonderful mother.'

I raised my eyebrows. 'You are, Love,' he said, patting my hand. 'And one day Moira will realise it and you two will be close again.'

'I hope so,' I said, appreciating his words.

'What would you have done instead,' he asked. 'If you hadn't met me?'

'I never knew,' I admitted. 'I didn't want to be a farmer's wife, but I never thought I'd leave Scotland.'

'You've my handsome face to thank for that,' he winked at me.

'Do you think,' I started, but hesitated. This conversation had been swirling in my mind for a while, but it never seemed the right time.

'Go on, say it,' he said, squeezing my arm gently.

'Do you think, when the children are grown and you've finished up at the business, do you think we might move back?'

'To Scotland?'

'Yes.'

'I never knew you missed it quite this much.'

'It's like an ache. It's like she's calling to me.'

'She?'

'Alba.'

He knew Alba was the Gaelic name, my mother often referred to our homeland as Alba.

'My darling,' he said, 'I'm so sorry.' His eyes glazed over.

'Don't be,' I said. 'I'm being silly. I adore you, and our life, and even though Moira drives me crazy, I adore our children.'

'Let's do it,' he said. 'I'll work in the business for a while, get things established with these new fellas. Then I'll find a job up there. Maybe I can work on the farm with Mal or find something to occupy me. We'll get you back to your homeland, my darling.'

That conversation filled me with hope. Hope that Moira would, as Tom predicted, grow out of this horrible phase. Hope that I'd be back in my beloved Scotland.

If I'd have known what little time I'd have with my children, what little years I had left, I might have done things differently. I might have been more patient, shared less opinions, let them be.

I would have cherished more of the little moments. I would have travelled more. Danced, and sang every day, and embraced life.

I'd have moved back to Scotland, before it was too late.

But I didn't know. I had no clue that my body was going to fail me.

I didn't fully appreciate that life is precious, and not a single moment should be wasted.

Chapter Nineteen

Marianne

The next day, we drove from Durness, down to Lochinvar and then on to Ullapool.

We'd worked out that it'd be about 90 miles, and take a few hours. However, we set aside the whole day so we could stop, enjoy the views, take photos, and just sit and be.

The landscape continued to be beautiful. Western Scotland never let us down with its beautiful beaches, clear turquoise water, green craggy hillsides, and quaint villages with white buildings and dormer windows. We saw 'heeland coos', deer, and lots of different birds.

It was raining lightly when we stopped for lunch, so we sat in the car, looking out over a gorgeous view. Finn pointed out a stag in the distance and we watched it mooching around, seemingly oblivious to our presence.

My phone buzzed, and I saw I'd received a video from my sister Tess.

'Want to watch it with me?' I asked Finn.

'Of course. So, you have two sisters?'

'Yes, Jane and Tess. They're both married and have two children each.'

I pressed play and felt myself fill with warmth as my three nieces and nephew filled the screen.

'Happy Birthday Aunty Marianne!' they said in chorus.

'Whoa, pause,' Finn said, astonished. 'It's your birthday?'

'I guess it is,' I said, laughing. 'I've lost all sense of the date and time.'

'You forgot?'

Okay, lovely Reader, of course I hadn't forgotten it was coming up. I just hadn't realised it was that day. I'd lost track of time. A handsome man and beautiful scenery does that to me. And I didn't want a fuss. I didn't want Finn to feel like we had to do anything special. I should have thought before I started the video. But here we were, now he knew.

I shrugged and pressed play.

'We miss you,' said my eldest niece, Zoe.

'And we hope you're having fun in Scotland,' said my nephew, little Alex.

'This is for your birthday,' said the youngest, Mabel, in her still-cute-baby voice.

They hesitated and all eyes drifted to Clare, who seemed to have forgotten her line.

'We love you!' said little Clare, grinning and blowing me a kiss.

My eyes were filling up. 'Aw they're so precious,' I said to Finn, my hand on my heart.

'Enjoy!' they said together, and then a photo slideshow started.

It was me, with them, at different times. In hospitals at each of their births, holding the tiny bundles of joy. Then various photos or clips throughout the years of me playing games, holding them as they slept on my lap, on day trips and outings.

My eyes misted over, watching all the lovely memories.

'Oh gosh,' I said, wiping my eyes. 'That was so lovely, bless them. Zoe, the eldest, is only seven.'

As I cleared my misty eyes, I realised Finn was looking at me in astonishment.

'What?' I asked, smiling to try and defuse the rising tension. He looked... *annoyed*.

'I thought you didn't like kids,' he said in an even tone.

'What? I never said that.'

'You don't want to have them.'

'No,' I said, pausing. 'I don't. That doesn't mean I don't love my nieces and nephews.'

'You're clearly great with them.'

'I adore spending time with them.'

'So why no kids of your own?'

I sighed. I'd had this conversation several times in the past. I didn't expect Finn to be one of the people to challenge me on this.

'I've never felt that urge. I love those kids fiercely and I'd do anything for them, but I also enjoy handing them back to their parents and going home to my own quiet, calm, low responsibility life.'

'Okay,' he said, nodding. 'I see.'

'I've had people ask me over and over again,' I told him, a slight edge to my voice. 'Especially after I got married. One woman I worked with said I clearly didn't like children. Another friend of my mother's said I was selfish not to have them.'

'Bloody hell, I'm sorry Marianne, that's awful.'

'I find it hard to explain,' I said, taking a deep breath and trying to find the words. 'I could give you a hundred reasons, like how humans are destroying the planet, and I don't feel the need to bring more children into it. That I prefer kittens to babies. I like my life as it is, being able to just take off and go on a trip like this, no big responsibilities. I've never felt that maternal urge that most women seem to have. But really, the reasons don't matter. I've never wanted to have a baby, and I shouldn't have to explain that choice to anyone.'

I almost added, 'including you', but stopped at the last minute.

'It's okay,' Finn said gently, but his tone was different; harder. Sadder. Perhaps he did like me more than I thought. Perhaps the realisation this couldn't go any further, when he wanted more kids, impacted him. Or perhaps, as a father, he took it personally. I didn't want to ask.

'You don't have to explain. People want to fit others into neat little boxes, they want things to be simple and easy to understand. It probably feels like a paradox to your family, that you love your nieces and nephews, yet don't want to have a baby yourself. But you can love them madly, enjoy their company, and still not want to be a mother yourself.'

He'd managed to understand me, and what I'd dealt with from others. I was both surprised and relieved at his words.

'Thank you, Finn. You seem to get it.'

'But I just want to say that you're clearly a fabulous aunt.'

I smiled. 'I try,' I said.

He smiled back, and I wondered what he was thinking but didn't want to ask.

'I guess the way to explain it is... I also love highland cows... but I don't want to open a cattle farm.'

He laughed. 'Fair enough.'

'Okay,' I said, changing the subject and pulling more food out for our lunch. 'Tell me something about you that I don't know already.'

He thought for a millisecond, then smiled.

'Okay, so when I was a kid, me and my sister used to have sandcastle building competitions. Every summer we'd go and stay with our grandparents. They lived near the sea, and we'd spend most of our time on the beach.'

'Sounds wonderful.'

'It was,' he smiled. 'They were great. And Clara and I got more and more competitive. We'd build sandcastles higher and higher. We'd decorate them with all sorts; shells, driftwood, seaweed, even litter. Clara was more artistic than me, but I was more ambitious in terms of height and size. Then we'd make our grandfather judge.'

'Love it, so who usually won?'

'Oh, it'd always be a draw. He'd say I came top in the architecture award, but she came top for creativity.'

'What lovely memories.'

'Yes.' He looked ahead at the view and shifted in his seat.

'Losing her must've been terrible.' I regretted saying it as soon as the words left my mouth.

'It was,' he said without a beat. 'But you know, I'm also very fortunate. I was lucky to have a great sister. And she lives on, in Iona.'

'Of course she does.'

'Tell me something I don't know about you.'

'Okay. Let me think.' I took a mouthful of salad, chewed, and came up with something. 'I can play the piano.'

'That's cool, are you any good?'

'I'm average,' I told him. 'I don't do it nearly enough, but I love it. I've got a piano, back home. Well, in a storage unit awaiting my next home.'

'I played a bit of violin when I was a kid,' he told me. 'I got bored quickly but wish I'd stuck with it.'

'Never too late to take up a new hobby,' I told him.

'That's very true. Okay, another random question. Do you have any pets?'

'Nope. Always wanted a cat but Ethan's allergic,' I told him. 'And now I think about it, that should've been a huge red flag. I love animals, how could I have married a man who would never be able to live with a pet! What was I thinking?'

We laughed.

'Well,' Finn said. 'That's the first thing you can do when you get settled somewhere new. Get a cat.'

'Oh, that's already the plan,' I said, smiling. 'In fact, I think I'll have two. How about you, have you ever had any pets?'

'Many dogs,' he told me, 'while I was growing up. Iona really wants a pet.'

'Well, as someone who was always told *no pets*, I think it's only fair you let her have one.'

'Oh, she'd love you for saying that,' he said, then looked down at the ground.

We cleared up our crumbs, and soon were back on the road.

Ullapool is a busy fishing village, with a small harbour, rows of white houses and gift shops. It even has a fish and chip shop with vegetarian options. We arrived early in the evening, found a hotel, purchased our fishless meal, and found a bench by the water looking out at the rocky coastline. It was a spectacular view, and I found myself wondering how I could ever contemplate not living in Scotland. I could drive to these places every weekend if I moved near my family in Lairg, or even if I lived near Luna in Inverness. A plan – a scary, almost crazy, but exciting plan – was coming together.

'Happy Birthday,' Finn said, holding up his can of Irn-bru, which I clinked with mine.

'Here's to friends with benefits,' I said, taking a swig. Finn laughed. 'This might be the best view I've ever had while I eat chips.'

'Best birthday I've ever had,' I said, hoping that didn't reveal too much. 'Great drive through stunning scenery, delicious meal out-doors, good company.'

'Aw you're sweet,' Finn said. 'I felt bad, thought you might have preferred to spend your birthday with your family.'

'Nah,' I said. 'Nieces and nephews excluded; my family aren't always super fun.'

I loved my family. Madly. But we were very different people.

'Your birthday isn't over yet,' he said, taking my rubbish from me. 'There's still super-hot birthday sex to look forward to. I'm going to rock your world tonight.' He winked, sending my head into a fizzy spin, and got up to walk to the bin.

I wasn't sure he could rock my world any more than he had already, without it tilting off its axis and killing me with too much pleasure. But I was looking forward to getting to the hotel room.

Finn sat beside me again and pulled a little paper bag out of his jacket pocket.

'Happy Birthday, sorry it's not wrapped.'

'Oh Finn,' I said, feeling choked. 'When did you get this?'

'While you were in the bathroom. I ran back to that gift shop we passed, I'm afraid this is the best I could do in the short time I had.'

'That's so sweet, thank you.'

Inside, there were three gifts. A bag of Scottish tablet, a tiny felt highland cow on a keyring, and a silver bracelet with a thistle charm.

'I love these, thank you,' I said, kissing him on the cheek. I took the bracelet out of its cellophane and held out my wrist while he put it on. Despite being naked with this man almost every day, I still felt a tingle as his fingers touched my wrist.

I attached the keyring to my keys, and we ate a few pieces of tablet, which was absolutely delicious; rich, creamy and sweet.

Our hotel that evening was a pub, so we decided to have a bottle of wine to celebrate my birthday. And then another. I was feeling quite tipsy, and about to suggest we went up to our room when a couple asked if they could join us. It was a small place and so we said yes and got chatting with them. Another bottle of wine appeared.

'We're on our honeymoon,' Penny, my new drunken friend told us. 'How about you?'

'Oh us, too,' Finn said, pulling me close and I stifled a giggle.

'Oh amazing,' said Kevin, Penny's new husband. 'When did you get married?'

I don't know why, or how we managed to be in sync, but we spun a story about how we married at Gretna and were doing the NC500 for our honeymoon. They asked how we met, and Finn answered without hesitation.

'Stirling Castle. It was love at first sight. She was talking to my daughter, and I had to stop and stare, she was just beautiful. I knew I had to get to know her better.'

I caught my breath.

'Then once we got to know each other, I just knew she was the one I'd been waiting for.'

'Oh, how romantic,' swooned Penny. 'I can see how in love you are.'

I glanced at Finn, who gave me a warm smile and put his arm around me. 'We're very happy,' he said. 'So how did you two meet?'

They told their story, but I zoned out. Suddenly, I felt sober and the fantasy we'd spun felt wrong and stupid. Why had we lied? For fun? Because in another, parallel universe that was what we wanted? What did all this mean and how did Finn really feel about me?

I was trying to find the words to admit the truth; that we weren't married, and in all honesty, had only known each other less than a month. But it was at that moment, Penny and Kevin said their goodbyes and left.

I couldn't cope with my rising anxiety. I wanted things to be simple and easy. I wanted to feel tipsy again. I wanted to get back to what we were good at: the physical side of our relationship.

Finn stood up. 'Another drink before closing? A birthday whisky perhaps?'

'To be honest,' I said, standing up. 'I just want to explore every inch of your body. Bedroom?'

He grinned. 'You drive me crazy,' he said, pulling my face to his and kissing me slowly, sending my whole body into a hot flurry of sensation.

We practically ran up the stairs, fumbled with the key and slammed the door shut before Finn pushed me against the wall, pulled my top over my head and had my bra off before I could blink. He started kissing my breasts, but I couldn't wait. I started begging, telling him I needed him, and I wanted him right now. Before I knew it, he was inside me, my back against the wall, my legs wrapped around his hips. He kept his eyes open, holding my gaze the whole time, the burning flesh of his body up against my own. It was the most intense, passionate sex of my life and I felt my climax building within minutes. He grinned as I lost all control, and I felt him come inside me as I cried out loud.

My legs slipped down from his hips, and he grinned at me as I giggled.

'We didn't even make it to the bed,' he said, smiling at me. 'Marianne, you drive me wild.' He kissed my neck, sending another flicker of excitement all the way through me.

'And you me,' I said, catching my breath as we moved away from the wall. 'I've been thinking about this all day.'

'Maybe we don't do an annual road trip,' he said, taking my hand and leading me to the bed. I held my breath. Was he suggesting we do this all year round?

'Maybe we just book a hotel for two weeks every summer and have as much sex as possible.'

He pulled me down on the bed, and we snuggled up, naked, under the covers.

'I think I could do this with you forever,' he whispered just before he fell asleep.

I just lay there, thinking about the story he'd told about how we met, wondering which parts were true.

Chapter Twenty

Marianne

I woke up the next day and felt like someone had smacked me over the forehead with a frying pan. Finn was asleep beside me, while I slipped out from under the covers and went for a shower. Deeply regretting not hydrating more the night before, I got dressed quietly, snuck out and bought a few large bottles of water. He was still asleep when I got back, so I sent a few replies to birthday texts and read one of the books I'd bought in Luna's shop for a while.

'Good morning,' he said as he sat up, rubbing his head. 'Oh Lord, we drank a lot. You're dressed, sorry are you waiting for me?'

'Only for breakfast,' I admitted. 'Not sure it's safe to drive just yet.'

He got up, walked naked to the bathroom and I let out a sigh. I wasn't sure I was enjoying this anymore. These feelings... this sense of loss before we'd even parted... the glimmer of something that would never be... it was all a bit much.

I blinked, and imagined myself feeling grounded to the spot, trying to focus on the moment. Before long, we were curing our hangovers with carbs; buttery toast, eggs, beans and mushrooms.

We were talking about everything and anything including Iona, my nieces and nephews, our food the night before and then Penny and Kevin.

'Nice couple, weren't they?' Finn said as he swigged the last of his coffee.

'You almost had me believing,' I said quietly. 'The story about how you saw me at Stirling Castle.' I gave a little laugh.

'Well,' he said, cocking his head. 'It was kind of true. I mean, I did see you, I did watch for a moment before I called Iona. I did think you were beautiful.'

I felt myself blush. 'Really?'

'Of course, really! I keep telling you how beautiful you are, how you drive me crazy with desire. You need to feel more sure of yourself, Marianne.'

I could only nod and smile.

'What made you say we were married?' I asked, not sure I wanted an answer within a millisecond of asking.

'I don't know,' he grinned. 'The wine, probably. Thought it'd be fun to make something up.'

'I felt a bit guilty by the end.'

'Yeah, me too.'

I remembered Penny saying we looked in love and opened my mouth to mention it but thought better of it. If I wanted to complete the trip, I needed to get things back to how they were; simple, easy, friendship with some hot sex thrown in for fun.

I popped to the bathroom and on the way back, couldn't resist stopping at a piano, tucked away in a corner. Mine was in storage and it'd been so long since I played. I prodded a few keys and the owner called over, telling me to help myself. I couldn't resist; I sat down and started to play.

Finn came over. 'Wow, you're really good.'

'I used to be part of an orchestra,' I told him. 'Many years ago.'

'I love that.'

'I'm a little out of practice,' I said, as my hands flew over the keys. I couldn't wait to get my own place, and get my piano set up. 'My mother taught me, and my sisters. She's a piano teacher.'

'That's awesome,' he said. It felt good that I'd impressed him, that he still had things to learn about me despite our intense amount of time together.

After returning to my seat, I got Grandad Tom's journal out of my bag. We looked at some of his photos in Ullapool, and then checked the next part of our journey.

'Applecross Pass today then,' Finn pointed to the map on his phone. 'I hear it's a great drive, really dramatic scenery.'

I was glad we were back to safe conversation. After hydrating and packing up, soon we were back on the road, enthusiastically talking about the stunning scenery, stopping to take photos and eat some Scottish tablet. After a few hours, we were at the start of Bealach na ba road, also known as the Applecross Pass. Finn told me to pronounce it *by-ee-alec-nuh-bah* and then laughed and rolled his eyes as I attempted to imitate his accent.

The road wound up through the mountains, climbing higher, with steep drops, crags covered in velvety green grass, and multiple small trickly waterfalls dotted about. We stopped at the summit, got out and took a few photos. It was breathtakingly beautiful.

'Lucky with the weather,' I said as Finn put his arms around me from behind. He'd become more and more affectionate; and the lines blurred once again in my head. Friends with benefits were friends who got close in the bedroom. He was treating me like his girlfriend. Not that I minded one bit. It was just the anticipation of losing him very soon that brought me down.

'I can't imagine doing this trip alone, thank you for agreeing to come with me,' he said quietly. I leaned my head back a little and he rested his chin on my head.

'Ditto,' was all I could manage. 'I'm having such a great time with you.'

'Me too.'

Applecross itself was a lovely place, and we got some lunch and had a walk along the beach. You could see over to the Isle of Skye. We talked a little about doing another trip, next summer, to the western isles. The idea filled me with joy, until Finn said, 'assuming we're both still single, of course.'

'I don't see myself falling in love again any time soon,' I said quietly. It'd take me a lifetime to get over these few weeks.

'It's a date, then.'

Our good luck with the weather finally ran out that afternoon, and we spent most of our time sitting inside a café, reading, talking and sipping hot drinks. I didn't mind; Scotland had already delivered more sunshine that I could have hoped for and as Finn reminded me; it wouldn't be so wonderfully green without the rain.

Finn's phone buzzed to life. 'Oh, it's my mum,' he said, answering. After greeting her, he started to frown.

'Oh, Mum.'

He was silent, listening for a bit and although I couldn't really hear her voice, I could tell she sounded stressed.

'Yes of course. I'll come and get Iona tomorrow, it'll take me all day to get to you though, I'm in Applecross.'

My eyes flicked to his and he looked so disappointed I reached out and touched his arm. So, this was it? The trip was over. What had happened?

'Okay, tell Dad I'm thinking of him. I'll call you tomorrow. Love you, Mum.'

He sighed as he put his phone down. By the look of despair on his face, I thought his dad must be seriously ill.

'I'm so sorry,' he said, scratching his head. 'It's my dad.'

'Is he okay?' I put my arm around him.

'Yes, he's okay but he's broken his leg.'

'Oh blimey, that's awful but I thought it was more serious, you looked distraught.'

He bit his lip. 'We need to cut our trip short. I feel I'm letting you down. If only you had your car, I'm sorry. But Mum can't cope with Iona on her own, Dad's having an op tomorrow and she's back and forth to the hospital.'

'It's okay, really,' I said, wondering what delights I'd miss out on then realising how selfish that was. 'Maybe we can finish the NC500 next year, before we head out to the islands.'

'You're amazing, thank you.' He kissed me on the hand.

'I guess you'll have to go straight to Stirling? Maybe you can drop me somewhere so I can get a train to Aviemore, then get back to my car?'

'Well, sure, yes or you could just come with me. We'll collect Iona and then you can come back home with us.'

I nodded. 'Sure, if you want me there.'

'I do. Marianne, I-'

His phone buzzed to life, his Mum again. 'Sorry.'

'It's fine.'

He answered, and I could hear Iona's sing-song voice. He had a little chat with her, while I thought about what I'd do – there were still places I wanted to visit from my grandad's journal, so I guessed I'd collect my car and come back to do those. The thought of travelling without Finn made me want to cry, but I managed to hold it together and felt calmer by the time he'd finished his call.

'It's stopped raining,' I pointed out. 'Shall we have a little walk before going to bed? Our last evening, we should be outdoors.'

We walked in silence for a bit, my arm linked with his, desperately trying to remember every moment, enjoying each minute of my time with him. We stopped to look out over the water. It was past 10pm, and the sun was on the horizon; the sky beautiful shades of golden yellow, bright oranges and fiery reds.

'This is my favourite moment,' I said. 'What a wonderful day, such gorgeous scenery and then capping it off with a sunset.'

'It's glorious,' he said, quietly.

'I bet you can't wait to see Iona.'

'Yeah, I feel terrible saying this, but I'm always grateful for a little break when she goes to either of her grandparents, and then I'm always thrilled when she comes back to me, too.'

'That's understandable. How long do you think it'll take us to get to her?'

'About five hours.'

I nodded.

'Marianne?' his tone was serious.

'Yes?' I took my arm from his and we faced each other. My heart was beating wildly.

'I just want to say, if things were different. If I didn't have Iona, or if you wanted children, and if you lived within an hour instead of in bloody England...'

I gulped.

'Yes?'

'If all those things weren't in our way, I'd want to be more than friends.'

'Me too,' I confessed.

'It's been fun pretending, though.'

A breeze blew my hair across my face, and he pushed it away.

'It has,' I agreed, wrapping my arms around him.

We didn't sleep much that night; making the most of being together, flesh on flesh, savouring every moment. Maybe we'd make it an annual trip, maybe we wouldn't. Right now, I just wanted to enjoy being with him, in the most physical way. Without a word, he seemed to feel the same, devouring me, touching every part of me, as I tried to commit him, his touch, and these feelings to my memory.

Wanting to get on the road early, we had a quick breakfast and planned our route east. Finn got a phone call, and wandered off while I was buying us some food for the journey.

'That was my uncle,' he said as we both got back into the car.

'Oh yeah?'

'He said he can bring Iona to me. He said there's no need to cut my trip short, he can meet us in Glencoe by teatime. What do you think?'

'How kind of him, that's fine by me.'

'He's great like that.'

'My grandparents visited Glencoe on their honeymoon, so I would really love to go there.'

'We talked about staying there for a few days, but obviously Iona will be with us now.'

His eyes were searching mine.

'What would you rather do?' I asked. On the one hand, I didn't want to end our trip early. On the other, Iona would completely change the dynamic. For a start, I assumed he'd be sharing a hotel room with her, not me, he could hardly leave her on her own in a strange room. And having a child in tow – though I loved my nieces and nephews – would make for a completely different time than being on our own.

'I think it's really up to you, this is your big trip.'

'Let's do it,' I said impulsively. 'It'll be fun.'

'You're sure?'

'Yes, we'll tell her we're friends, right? As you said she might get the wrong idea, we don't want her getting her hopes up about you finding a girlfriend.'

Something flickered in his eyes, but he just nodded, and he rang his uncle back to hatch a plan.

The journey from Applecross to Glencoe was one of the most scenic drives of the trip. We went inland, passing lochs and gorgeous green scenery. We chatted like always but something had shifted; we knew we wouldn't be sharing a bed tonight. Despite all the talk of doing another road trip in future, I doubted we'd ever do this again and the sadness was overwhelming. I tried to focus on the land, on Finn's conversation, on looking out for deer and searching on my phone for a place to stay in Glencoe.

'How about a cottage?' I asked, finding a nice little place with a view of Loch Leven. 'Three bedrooms. I can only book it for three nights minimum, but I'm happy with that, if you want to stay a few days?'

'Sounds great,' he said. 'There's plenty to do around there.'

We detoured to Glenfinnan Viaduct, also known as the Harry Potter bridge, a film location for the Hogwarts Express. We walked up and underneath the impressive structure, then down to the shores of Loch Shiel. As with the rest of the trip, it was beautiful and green. I felt at peace. It started to rain, but we didn't mind, walking and talking about everything and anything. Anything except what was at the forefront of my mind: how much I was going to miss him.

'Thank you for doing this with me,' I told him, as we looked up at the viaduct for one last moment. 'I know we haven't done the exact NC500 route you planned.'

'I think your grandad's journey has been the perfect guide. And thank you, it's been a pleasure.'

'I mean it though,' I said, turning to him. 'This has been more than a friendship.' My heart beat faster, afraid to say too much but knowing I needed him to understand what this had meant to me. This might be my last chance before Iona was with us. 'More than sex buddies. More than travel companions. You've helped me to heal and to understand myself better. To grow and move on from the version of me that, honestly, was broken just a year ago. Thank you isn't nearly enough.' My eyes misted up.

He smiled and hugged me. 'You've helped me more than you'll ever know, too.' He pulled away. 'My life has revolved around Iona, work, and the occasional bit of fun. You've helped me to open up, to feel intimate with someone. To appreciate the beauty of Scotland so much more than if I'd done this alone.'

We looked at each other for a few moments, taking in all we'd said and holding in so much more.

'We'd better get going,' I said eventually. 'Iona will be on her way by now.'

He hesitated, opened his mouth to speak but then stopped. We got back in the car.

I could see immediately why Grandad loved Glencoe. A gorgeous dramatic green valley, with waterfalls, lochs, and clean, fresh air. We drove all around the area, me saying 'oh wow' every five minutes. The village itself, where our cottage was, was lovely, with a handful of amenities and the shores of gorgeous Loch Leven.

I was throwing a bunch of our clothes into the washing machine in the quaint kitchen when I heard a car pull up outside. I felt anxious; was I just intruding on what could have been a little holiday for Finn and his daughter? What would she make of me being here, and how about the uncle?

I went to the doorway and saw Iona running into Finn's arms.

'Daddy!'

'Hi baby girl,' he said, lifting her high and swinging her around.

The walking, talking, beautiful, sweet girl, who we'd spoken about so much, was here and while I was pleased for her and Finn… everything would be different now. Her red hair flew out around her face as she beamed with happiness to see him. It was a lovely sight, and I couldn't help but feel warm inside watching them.

Vic, his uncle, got out and they shook hands. 'Thanks for this,' Finn told him. 'Really good of you.'

'Seemed a shame to cut your trip short,' he said. He looked over at me. 'You must be Marianne, nice to meet you.' He held out his hand and I shook it.

Vic came in and we gave him a cup of tea and a sandwich before he travelled back to Stirling. He assured Finn he'd help out his parents and there was no need to worry.

Iona was full of beans, telling us what she'd been up to; about how Grandpop had fallen off a wall, how she'd cried, and how she found the ambulance exciting. She was full of energy and joy.

'I'll walk down to the village store,' I said, getting up, 'see if I can get us something for our dinner, maybe some pasta?'

I thought I'd give them some time alone, but Iona jumped up.

'Can I come? I can help.'

'Why don't we all go,' Finn said, reaching for his shoes.

'No Daddy, we need girl time,' Iona grinned. 'You can get the table ready for dinner.'

He laughed. 'Can I now? Is that okay with you, Marianne?'

'Of course.'

As Iona and I walked down the road, I asked her about herself; her hobbies, her friends, her school. We were almost at the shop when she started asking about me; what my favourite colour was and if I enjoyed my holiday.

'It's nice to see my dad with a woman,' she said as we looked around the store.

'Oh really?' I said, laughing.

'Well, that's what my Nana said. She said *it's about time.*'

I laughed awkwardly. Good to know they were all talking about me.

'Can we have pesto?' Iona asked, holding up a jar. 'Daddy likes it and so do I.'

'Pesto it is then, and some garlic bread?'

Loaded up with dinner, breakfast, items to make packed lunches and enough snacks to feed the whole village, we headed back, laden with carrier bags. I was glad she'd come; she was stronger than she looked and offered to carry some of it for me.

'Isn't it beautiful here,' I said, looking out over the loch.

'It is.' Iona stopped for a moment and put the bags by her feet. 'What's your favourite bird?'

'Hmm...' I thought for a moment. 'I really like blue tits,' I said. 'Where I used to live, some were nesting in my garden.'

'Aw that's cute.' Iona seemed impressed.

'What's your favourite bird?'

'Well,' she said, enthusiastically. 'I love puffins. But I also really like eagles. My Nana loves birds, and she said her favourite is a woodpecker.'

'All good choices,' I said. 'Puffins are very cute.'

'What do you think Daddy's favourite will be?'

'Let's ask him.' We continued back to the cottage.

I was looking forward to tomorrow's trip so much more than I had that morning. Iona was bubbly and fun, and I could manage to keep my hands off Finn for a few days. Just about.

'My friend Ella came here on holiday,' Iona told me. 'She went up a ski lift. Can we do that?'

'Sounds good to me,' I said. 'Let's see if we can find out where it is.'

'Ella was mean to me last time I saw her, so when we go back to school, I can tell her I've been to see the places she went to, and maybe she'll like me again.'

I slowed the pace and asked more questions about her friend. Iona told me lots of positive stories, but it was clear this girl Ella had a mean streak.

'Why do you think Ella is cruel sometimes?'

Iona shrugged. 'I don't know.'

'What's life like for her at home?'

'Well, her mummy and daddy got divorced and she doesn't see her mummy much.'

'That's got to be very hard for her, maybe that's why she isn't always nice. Maybe she's sad inside?'

'But I don't even remember my mummy, and I'm not mean to people.'

'But imagine if you'd had a lovely mummy around all the time, then she was suddenly gone. That might be quite hard to deal with.'

'So maybe Ella is sad and that makes her grumpy and mean?'

'Exactly. Maybe you could ask her, gently, if she wants to talk about it.'

'Talk about what?' Finn asked as he opened the door.

'Marianne thinks Ella is sad, so I'm going to try and help her feel less sad and then maybe she'll be less mean.' Iona said this like it was obvious and pushed past him into the kitchen.

'It's a long story,' I said, smiling at him. We'd only been apart for a half hour or so, but my heart swelled as he smiled back at me.

We made dinner together, ate popcorn in front of the television, and after Iona had fallen asleep in her pyjamas on the sofa, Finn carefully carried her up to bed.

'Thank you,' he said when he came back down.

'For what?'

'That Ella thing has been going on for ages, but she's just said she thinks she can make it better.'

'Well, that's good, I hope it helps. Cup of tea?' I stood up, ready to go to the kitchen.

'I noticed something,' he said, a wicked glint in his eyes.

'Oh yeah?'

'There's a lock on your bedroom door. I mean... if we were very quiet...'

I practically threw myself on him.

Chapter Twenty-One

Nora. 1981

It felt like I had my babies, blinked, and then they left home. Frank went off to university to study architecture and begin his career in that field. Everyone said how clever he was, and we were ever so proud of him.

Moira, by contrast, continued to disappoint. She drank too much, left the shoe company and got a job behind a bar. There was nothing wrong with that, but I'd hoped she'd have ambition to do more. Women had more options, more power, more choices than ever before and I wanted her to live to her full potential.

Her boyfriend, Ricky, had been on the scene for several years and I had no idea what she saw in him. He jumped from job to job, got into fights, and had too much to say about what my daughter did.

For the sake of peace, I kept my opinions to myself, and eventually she left to go and live with him in a damp, cold flat near Northampton. We bought them furniture, and sometimes I'd invite them for a Sunday roast. But we didn't see much of her for a while.

The sale of the shoe business went through, and Tom stayed on, managing the merger of his family-run business into a large corporation. He seemed to thrive, and the money from the sale paid off our mortgage. I continued to bake; wedding and birthday cakes being my specialism.

It was a new phase for us, with an empty nest, but life felt calm. Moira was off doing her own thing but at least I wasn't witness to it. Frank was very independent. Tom was happy.

When my mother died, I returned home for a few weeks. It's funny, I always referred to the farm as home, as though the house we lived in was only temporary.

Between helping Mal with administration, spending time with the family, and meeting friends, I was very busy. But I found time to walk the hills, to ground myself. It was like every visit re-charged me.

My mother and I hadn't been super close for most of my adult life. She'd refused to come and visit us, never keen to cross the border into England, but I forgave her that year. I accepted her choices, and made peace with them. Now she wasn't here to talk to, I found myself whispering to her when in my bed, or while walking along in the fields. I'd tell her little stories about my life, or remember details from my childhood. I felt like she hadn't left me, in spirit. In a weird way, I felt closer to her during that time than I had for years. She was at peace, and I was at peace with our relationship.

I started to think about where I'd like to live if Tom and I carried out our plan. He'd want some part-time work, and I would like to keep baking. Perhaps we could be a little further south, not in a big city like Glasgow or Edinburgh, but Inverness. I spent an hour one afternoon staring at the map, looking at villages, wondering what they'd be like. Tom had told me the Cairngorms were beautiful. Maybe we could settle somewhere near there. We could work in Inverness and drive into the Cairngorms for nice walks at the weekend, or up to my home village of Lairg, to see Mal and his family.

Frank and Moira would visit. Maybe we'd get a new pet. I fancied a cat.

My mind continued, making plans, day-dreaming about our home, our lifestyle, the life we'd create for ourselves.

I told Mal my ideas, and he asked if I regretted leaving.

I shrugged. 'Tom had his family business to run. We didn't have any choice.'

'You chose to marry him.'

'It didn't feel like a choice,' I admitted. 'I was so in love with him. Still am, luckily.'

'Then it was worth it.'

It was. Tom was my great love story, my soul mate, my life. But my heart also belonged to Scotland, and she'd been calling me back ever since I'd left. I didn't want to wish time away, but I couldn't wait to make the big move back.

When I got home, I shared it all with Tom, even down to the last detail about the pets we'd have, and how I'd decorate our new home. He was full of encouragement and said we'd do it within the next ten years.

Don't wait, Reader. Don't wait to pursue your dream.

Chapter Twenty-Two

Marianne

After very-quiet-but-just-as-amazing sex, Finn snuck back to his room in case Iona wanted him in the middle of the night. It took me a long time to get to sleep, my emotions at an all-time high.

This was too quick, too fast to feel such strong feelings, surely? We were in a nice little bubble, in a holiday fantasy land, but I needed to get things into perspective.

Sure, maybe given time, with the right location and a different set of circumstances, Finn and I would get together, make a home together, and have a very nice life. But there was no point in lingering on *what ifs*. I resolved to keep my feelings in check, keep it real, have fun with him and Iona the next few days and then be on my way.

As sleep was escaping me, I got out my iPad and did some research.

That I'd live anywhere but Scotland was out of the question. This land had called to me for years and this trip did not disappoint. Even when it was wet and windy, I would rather be here than anywhere else. Whether it was an ancestral thing, or a love of green hills and mountains, or the quiet solitude of the rural areas...or a combination of all these things, I had no doubt this was where I belonged.

There were yoga and meditation teacher classes I could do online, I could complete the training, find a part-time job, build up some sort of wellness business. I even considered teaching piano; I'd been good enough to play professionally at one point and I yearned to get that good again. Next, I researched places to live in or near Inverness. Luna and I had been texting or speaking almost every day, and the thought of living where I knew at least one person was appealing. She'd also mentioned she needed help in her shop, so she'd be my first port of call to find work. It would help me pay my bills while I grew my business.

And maybe, now and then, when he had a babysitter, Finn and I would get together for a night of fun. He'd only be 45 minutes' drive away. I didn't mention my ideas to him, or even to Luna, as they were still swirling, forming in my mind. Plus, lovely though they sounded, it was a new life, new place, new friends, and new career. I needed a bit more time to think it through.

I looked at other ways I could make money, as well as teaching yoga. I was interested in all sorts but one topic I was fascinated in was the law of attraction. Maybe I could teach it, or coach on it, or *something*. I wasn't sure yet but, in the meantime, I read as much as I could. One tool for manifesting your desires was to visualise exactly what you want, in every tiny colourful detail.

I would create a new life here. I would put down roots in Scotland, which was already my spiritual home, but would soon be my physical home, too. The thought filled me with joy.

I closed my eyes and pictured it; I woke up in a comfortable bed, in an old, but cosy, stone cottage in a rural village. I started my day with breakfast, and stretches, and a short walk in the lovely Scottish hills surrounding my home. Then I'd get back, and I'd have appointments, mostly online, teaching mindfulness and meditation techniques, coaching and mentoring others on their wellbeing. I'd write a blog and make video content. I'd hold a yoga class in the nearby village hall on Tuesday evenings. Luna and I would get together regularly for dinner, wine, and meaningful conversation.

It all felt so real, so vivid in my mind, that I couldn't help smiling.

I pictured myself at the end of one of these days, getting dinner prepared. Finn and Iona were in the kitchen.

I blinked my eyes open. Finn and Iona were there?

Telling myself it was just a harmless fantasy, I went with it.

After we shared a lovely meal, Finn read a bedtime story to Iona while I fed our cat and tidied up. Then we'd make passionate love, fulfilling every wanton pleasure, hungry for each other as we ever were.

I fell into a deep sleep, finally at peace.

I awoke at 8am, stretched and looked outside, pleased to see it was sunny. I opened my bedroom door and went downstairs to make coffee.

Iona had got up before Finn. Together, we made sandwiches and for our day out. I asked her questions about her life, and she chatted away. I learned a lot of facts about puffins. And then she asked me questions about my favourite animals.

We found a common interest in our love of all things feline. We talked for a while about cats and agreed that Finn must be persuaded to let her adopt a rescue cat. We discussed names, and how she'd have to brush her new pet, play with it, and help feed it. I said something about picking up its poo in the litter tray and she fell about laughing, as I knew she would. My nieces found the word 'poo' hilarious at that age.

We were eating cereal and talking about big cats, (I loved cheetahs while she was a fan of snow leopards), when Finn appeared in the kitchen doorway, his hair sticking up in random places. He looked sleepy but sexy as ever. I wanted to go over, kiss him and take him back to bed. I could tell by the way he was looking at me that he was thinking the same thing.

Iona got up, ran over to him and gave him a hug. She told him all about the plans to get a cat, which he sounded fairly open to, but when Iona went upstairs, he said 'looks like I'm getting a cat, thanks for that.'

'You're welcome,' I winked as I went up to get ready. 'You won't regret it, cats are awesome.'

Glencoe Lochan is a mini loch. It's an easy, flat walk, the shores lined with trees and stunning mountains including the glorious Pap of Glencoe.

We walked slowly, taking photos and talking. Iona pointed out particular trees, insects, birds, flowers, shadows, cloud shapes and everything else. She often skipped ahead, Finn and I envious of her energy and admiring her enthusiasm for the natural world.

We sat on logs to eat our lunch and when we stood up to walk on, Finn slipped his hand into mine. I looked at him, wondering if it was by accident, but he just gave me a warm smile, and squeezed. It took Iona a few minutes to notice because she'd been fascinated by a bird of prey she'd been watching.

I saw her eyes move from our hands to Finn's face, and then mine, and she broke into a big grin and skipped along, without a word. I didn't want her to get her hopes up, to think this was more than it was, and had no idea what Finn was playing at, risking her getting hurt like that, but I also couldn't bear to pull my hand away.

We stopped for a while at a small wooden jetty, Iona insisting we were silent so that she could try and spot some wildlife. She sat crossed-legged while Finn and I stood behind her, still holding hands.

'I love it here,' I whispered to him.

'Me too, beautiful isn't it.'

'Imagine living in Glencoe, you could come here every day for a walk. Then go into the mountains or visit the sea at the weekends.'

'I can see you here,' he said. 'I can also see you where we live, enjoying the Cairngorms, visiting the beaches not too far from us.'

My eyes flew to his. He was looking at me intently. Iona told us to 'sshh' and pointed across the water, where some deer had come to drink.

We watched, magnetised. As they wandered off, Finn started to say how cool it was, but Iona told him to wait, as she watched a dragonfly dance across the water.

I looked up at him and smiled. He turned towards me and kissed me gently on the forehead. Iona didn't appear to notice, mesmerised by the dragonfly.

We let her watch for a while before encouraging her to move on. Back at the car, she was still buzzing and chatting about everything we'd seen.

'It's great you love the outdoors,' I told Iona. 'A lot of children would get bored going for walks.'

'That's weird,' she said. 'I love being outside.'

'Everyone's different, my wee Hen,' Finn ruffled her hair.

'Dad, you'll ruin my hair.'

I'd helped her plait her hair that morning. 'Sorry,' he said, winking at her as she got into the car.

'It's okay. So, when will we get the cat?'

'Do your seatbelt up,' he said, giving me a pointed look. 'We'll talk about it when we get home to Aviemore.'

'Marianne, will you help us find one?'

Finn looked at me, waiting just as much as Iona for my answer.

'Maybe,' I said. 'We'll see.'

'I hope so,' she said.

I realised, with alarm, that I hoped so too.

From there, we went for a drive, showing Iona what we'd seen the day before. Like us, she was in awe of the valley and the views. Even though they'd both lived close to the Cairngorms, which was a stunning place, they appreciated everywhere they saw, and their enthusiasm was infectious.

We got out of the car to have a look around and walked along a river. We stood at the bank; Iona and I threw pebbles into the water while Finn sat on a large boulder, watching us, smiling. She was hopeful to see more deer, and we passed some in the car on the way back. Finn slowed right down, and we put our windows down. There were three, grazing, but each lifted its head to look at us for a moment.

'Aren't they lovely,' whispered Iona.

'Sure are, sweetie,' I agreed. 'You know, you could work with animals when you're grown up.'

'I could be a vet!' she said, as Finn pulled away slowly.

'Or you could work at a zoo,' I suggested.

'Ooh yes, or I could work with snow leopards in the wild!'

'That would be amazing,' I said. 'I'll come visit you.'

'Okay and when you arrive, I'll make you a nice dinner.'

'Sounds wonderful, thank you.'

'What do you do for a job, Marianne?'

Finn looked up. 'Actually, I don't really know this either.'

'Well, I did work for an insurance company,' I told them. 'Do you know what insurance is?'

Iona shook her head, and so Finn gave her a simple summary.

After he'd given her a child-friendly explanation I said, 'I decided how big a risk there was, to work out what sort of insurance my company could offer people.'

'What made you want to do that,' Iona said. 'It sounds a bit boring.'

'Iona, that's rude!' Finn said as I laughed.

'Sorry,' she said.

'To be honest, it was a bit boring,' I admitted. 'I was good with numbers, and analysing information. I didn't know what to do with my life so I just ended up doing it. I was good at it, so I did well. It didn't occur to me to stop and ask if it was interesting or boring.'

'And then you did, and it was boring, so you left?'

'Exactly. And now I need to find a new job. I've got some ideas, but I'm not sure yet what I'd be good at.'

'I think you'd be good at anything,' she said, smiling broadly.

'Aw, thank you. I think you'd be good at anything too.'

Back in the village, we made some dinner, and ate together, talking about our day, interspersed with some snow leopard facts which Iona made Finn find on his phone. It was only after Iona fell into bed, exhausted, that the day went wrong.

It was a warm evening, and we took a bottle of wine out into the tiny back garden. Iona's bedroom was at the front of the house, but we kept our voices low so as not to wake her.

'I've had the best day,' I said, taking a sip of my wine. 'Iona is great, you should be really proud of her.'

'Thank you, I am.'

'I love it here, just wonderful.'

'Have you thought any more about what you're going to do when this is over?'

I looked at him, and for the first time since we'd met, he looked nervous.

'Well, I know for sure I'm going to live in Scotland,' I told him, staring into the trees at the back of the garden. 'I feel connected here, like this is my home, and I want to set up my own business. I want to teach meditation and mindfulness, yoga, reiki, all sorts of wellness and spiritual topics. Maybe I could even organise spiritual mindfulness retreats in the Highlands.'

'That's fantastic,' he grinned and asked more questions. Ethan's eyes had glazed over whenever I'd spoken about my interests in the mind, body, spirit arena. He'd been cynical, and uninterested. Finn was almost the exact opposite, taking an interest, sharing his thoughts and ideas, encouraging me to embrace this passion and make it into a business.

'I'll need a job to start with though,' I said, 'I'll need income while I build the business. Luna needs help in her shop so I could find a place not too far from Inverness, and work part-time with her, if she'll have me.'

He smiled. 'That's not too far from me, either.'

'Nope,' I smiled at him. 'Perfect for the occasional overnighter when you've got a babysitter.'

His face changed.

'So, you'd only want to see me at night, and when Iona isn't around?'

I was taken aback.

'No, sorry that's not what I meant.'

'Is she so terrible?'

'Finn!'

He looked down at the ground. 'Forget it.'

'No, what do you mean? I've been super nice to her all day.'

'You've been great with her.'

'So, what's the problem?'

'There's no problem. I'm tired, I think I'll just go to bed.' He got up, putting his half-drunk glass of wine down on the table.

'Finn? Come on, sit down, let's talk about this.'

I was saying the words, but I didn't want to talk. There was no solution here. No romantic happy ending.

'I think it's best we leave it.'

'Finn!' I stood up, went to him, and put my hand on his chin, forcing him to look me in the eye. 'Finn, I just meant, we could still be friends with benefits. That's all.'

He looked at me intensely, his eyes burning.

'Of course,' he said, and then he kissed me, hard. We took our wine to bed. But instead of intense, fiery, can't-control-ourselves sex, this time it was slow, and loving... and it felt like a goodbye.

Chapter Twenty-Three

Marianne

The next day we went to Aonach Mòr, the mountain with the ski lift which Iona's friend Ella had talked about. It was actually an enclosed gondola. I drove, and Finn read out some random details on the way, including the fact that Aonach Mòr is Britain's eighth highest mountain. Iona thought that was pretty awesome.

The gondola takes you 650 metres high, where you can walk on fairly even ground and see spectacular views in every direction, including the summit of Ben Nevis, the tallest of them all. Finn had climbed Ben Nevis before and Iona asked him lots of questions about it as we approached in the car.

As we parked, I tried to imagine Aonach Mòr covered in snow, with people skiing, and decided I'd have to come again in the winter. I'd never skied, but I'd also never quit my job and headed north for a road trip solo holiday, nor had a friend with benefits. So I was sure I could manage to learn to ski, too. My new-found bravery buoyed me as we got out of the car. How far I'd come from my magnolia-tree-staring, binge-eating days.

We joined a short queue to get into our gondola, a small metal cabin that rocked slightly, and was on a continuous loop.

'I'm scared,' Iona said, looking up at the mountain. 'Maybe we shouldn't go. What if we fall? Or what if it gets stuck and we're trapped inside?'

Finn crouched down in front of her. 'We'll be fine, they wouldn't let people ride if it wasn't safe.'

'People have to get on very quickly, it doesn't stop for you,' she pointed towards the front of the queue, where people were stepping on.

'Just hold your mum's hand,' said a well-meaning lady in front of us, smiling at me.

Iona's eyes flew to mine. 'Can I hold your hand?'

'Why don't you hold both of our hands?' I suggested, as we stepped a little closer.

She took mine, and then Finn's as he stood up. I wondered if others noticed us, assuming we were a conventional family. A mother, a father and a daughter, out for a ride up the mountain.

For a moment, I felt whole.

I felt like this was exactly where I was meant to be. With this wonderful man, and his lovely daughter. We stepped onto a platform, and Iona squeezed my hand tighter.

'You've got this,' I said. 'Sometimes, you have to face your fears, and I promise the views at the top will be worth it.'

'I've got this!' she shouted as we stepped forward. Finn got in first and pulled her in with him, me stepping in last. We all giggled as we found our seats and the gondola swayed a little.

'Eek!' she squealed, smiling. 'That was scary.'

'But you did it!' I said, giving her a high five. She grinned, sat beside me, and turned to the window. I looked at Finn, who was smiling warmly at me.

I thought back to what he'd asked me the night before, was Iona "so terrible?"...was he hinting that it wasn't so bad to have children? Iona was wonderful, but I still didn't want a baby and he clearly did. There was no future here. I took a big, deep breath. No more fantasising.

This would never work. It'd be just like when I was with Ethan; he'd start hinting, I'd feel guilty, he'd feel resentful, and the whole thing would fall apart.

Remembering the reality of the situation would make it easier for me to leave in a few days and get on with my life. We weren't compatible when we clearly wanted very different things.

I turned to the window, the view getting better and better as we ascended, Iona pointing out trees she liked, a loch in the distance, hikers with their dogs. She was nervous again as we reached the top and Finn held out his hand, but she took mine.

'Marianne will help me,' she said, squeezing me tight. Finn got off first and we hopped off behind, and then she didn't let go of me as we walked, until she saw the gift shop and said something about spending pocket money. Finn and I hovered in the entrance as she browsed.

'You okay?' I asked Finn, who watched her intently.

'I just like seeing you two together,' he said. 'It makes me a little sad, if I'm honest.'

'For the record,' I said, feeling our conversation last night was unresolved. 'Iona isn't terrible. She's wonderful. She's bright, full of life, and I've enjoyed time with her. It doesn't mean I want to have lots of babies.'

'Who said anything about having babies?' he looked at me, confusion in his eyes.

'Everyone!' I said, feeling frustrated. 'My family, friends, colleagues, my soon-to-be ex-husband. They all expect me to have a baby, like there's something wrong with me for making that life choice. I can enjoy spending time with Iona without wanting a kid of my own.'

'Understood.' Finn said, looking away. 'I hear you loud and clear.'

He moved away, into the shop and I watched him go over to Iona. She showed him a few things she wanted, and he gently persuaded her that she had enough stuffed toys, but that the book about insects was a great choice. I hovered in the doorway, feeling myself emotionally step back from Finn. I felt tears forming behind my eyes. We were days away from separating and I couldn't be miserable. I wanted to enjoy every moment, commit it to my memory and savour it while I could.

We walked for a while, the terrain rugged and beautiful, the vistas breath-taking. Finn and I fell back into easy conversation about the area. He used his phone to figure out which mountain was on the horizon, and to locate lochs and milestones in the distance. Iona ran ahead, fascinated with nature, from the bugs on the ground, to the insects in the air (even the horrible midge that bit me), to the grasses, trees, lochs, valleys and mountains. She told us facts, asked questions and at one point held my hand again for a bit. I glanced at Finn, and saw him look at our hands, then he quickly moved his eyes away into the distance.

When it was time to go back down, Iona bravely stepped back into the gondola unassisted and we gave her a mini round of applause. She sat next to me again, and leaned on my shoulder, yawning loudly.

'Holidaying is very tiring,' she said. I put my arm around her, and she snuggled in. I avoided eye contact with Finn.

Back at the cottage, Finn got a phone call from his mum, and during the conversation, it was clear his dad was out of surgery. Iona suddenly ran out into the garden, so I went after her and found her crying. She'd clearly been worried about her grandad and was relieved. I comforted her the best I could and by the time Finn joined us, she was wiping the last of her tears.

'It's okay Daddy,' she said, giving him a hug. 'I was upset about Grandad, but Marianne made me feel better.'

He gave me a look, as if to say, yet again – *but you're good with her...* which I ignored. I was also good at baking; it didn't mean I'd make a good bakery owner, or more importantly, want to. I was a strong swimmer, but it didn't mean I wanted to swim competitively. The list went on, but I didn't say anything, just let my mind spin around the confused feelings, for him, for Iona, for life.

We drove into Fort William, picked up Chinese food, took it back and ate it in the garden with our coats on, making the most of the dry weather, even though it was a little cool.

'Today was the best day of my life,' said Iona, sitting back in her chair with a big grin on her face.

'It was pretty awesome, Wee Hen,' Finn winked at her.

'I can't believe how high we went in the gondola! And Grandad's feeling better. And now this yummy dinner!'

'I think it was one of my best days, too,' I said, squeezing her arm. I meant it.

I contemplated it for a moment as we sat around the table; I could, if they'd have me, have a life with these two. I was falling for her, for him, for both of them, for the idea of the three of us together. Finn said Iona spent time with both sets of grandparents. I'd have fun with her when she was around, and Finn and I would also get time alone when she wasn't. I could be an aunt, like I was to my niece and nephews, but live-in. I could.

But did I want to? The conflict of emotion confused me, scared me, and made my head swirl. And then it dawned on me. She didn't need an aunt. She deserved someone who was all-in, committed, who wanted to be a mother-figure, who was willing to adopt her wholeheartedly the way Finn had, and I wasn't the woman to do that. I'd never had that maternal urge and I couldn't force it. She deserved better.

I looked at Finn as he was making a joke with his chopsticks, putting them in his mouth and saying he was a walrus. Iona was in fits of giggles.

He'd also reacted oddly the few times I'd mentioned I didn't want to have a baby. He'd questioned me, I remembered. He'd wanted to be sure. So, he clearly wanted more children and, I reminded myself, this was another reason it could not work.

If he didn't have Iona. If he wanted a child-free life... Would things be different?

Yes. Yes, they would.

My breath caught for a moment with the depth of my feelings for him.

But then again, I questioned myself, were they real? It'd been intense; being together all the time had sped everything up. I'd thought I was in love with Ethan, once. I'd thought that was forever. I'd ended up depressed, lonely, and on the brink of wanting to end my life. Relationships failed, and when they did, it was awful.

I thought back to my time right after Ethan, how I'd decided I wouldn't fall in love again. The pain of breaking up when you'd expected it to be forever was too great. I imagined talking to Luna, and I knew what she'd say.

She'd tell me what I'd tell any friend; that love was worth a risk. That every time was different. That we had to face our fears, just like Iona had faced her fear and got on the gondola.

I watched Finn and Iona, messing around, eating their food, and I once again pictured myself doing this every day.

But one big thing was still in the way. Even if I could get around the fear. Even if I could consider being a parent to Iona of some sort...

I still didn't want a baby. Not because of fear, I simply hadn't wanted to and never would. I never got that broody feeling women talked about. I didn't see myself having a baby, and never had.

I couldn't give him what he wanted, or deprive him of that choice, when clearly, he was a wonderful father.

So, that was the end of it. Maybe it'd be for the best if I didn't get any closer, that we didn't stay in touch as friends, with or without benefits. It was best to end it before anyone got hurt. I resolved to leave soon after we got back to Finn's house. Just a few more days, and then I'd get on with my life.

Finn took Iona up to bed while I washed up. After I'd put all the dishes away, I needed the bathroom and started up the stairs when I overheard a conversation not meant for my ears. I should have retreated but I was frozen, wanting to hear every word.

'But you really, *really* like each other,' Iona was saying.

'Marianne and I are just friends, as I told you before.'

'A very good friend.'

'Truthfully? She's my best friend.'

My breath caught.

'Even more than your friend Greg?'

Finn laughed lightly. 'Yes, even more than Greg.'

'I really like her.'

'I know, me too.'

'Maybe you love her.'

There was a silence, and I held my breath. I really needed the bathroom, should I just continue up the stairs? I didn't want Finn to find me eavesdropping.

'Please don't wish for things that might not happen, Iona.'

I kept going up the stairs, which creaked and alerted them to my presence.

'Good night, sweet dreams.'

'Good night, Daddy.'

Might. *Might not happen?* So, it might happen, it might not? That one word 'might' would play on my mind for the rest of the evening.

Chapter Twenty-Four

Nora. 1985

Moira came to her senses one cold February day, when she arrived on my doorstep, with all her bags, her mascara smudged and her eyes wet. I welcomed her in with a hot cup of sugary tea, a plate of homemade biscuits, and lots of hugs.

Ricky had knocked her confidence and she couldn't seem to make simple decisions. It took a while, but after a few months she asked Frank to teach her some basic computer skills and she got a job in an office as a typist. After years of worry, I finally felt she could create a good future.

'I'm sorry about my evil years,' she said to me one day, and I just hugged her.

'You were never evil,' I told her, welling up. 'Just a little unpleasant at times.'

'Almost evil, then,' she said, laughing lightly.

That same year, Frank met Orla and brought her home to introduce us. She was confident, taught piano, and loved reading. She talked to me for hours while we baked a cake and prepared a roast dinner. I knew from that day she loved my son; she was so full of praise for him, his career, his kindness to her and she talked a lot about their future together. She talked about Jane Austen and Thomas Hardy and told me she'd name my grandbabies after great characters from her favourite books.

Tom was starting to wind things up at work. We agreed he'd resign the following year and we'd put the house on the market. Moira said she'd come with us to Scotland, and Frank was supportive, promising to visit with Orla as much as they could.

We lost my dear mother-in-law that year. Other than Tom, she'd been my anchor, my guide as a mother, a true friend when I'd started this life in the south, and I felt the loss greatly.

She was born in Cornwall, so that summer we all went there for a week, with Orla too. We rented caravans and spent our time walking along the cliff tops, relaxing on the beach, paddling in the sea, and eating fish and chips and Cornish pasties.

Frank and Orla moved in together shortly after that. Moira got her own flat, leaving me again with an empty nest. However, this time it felt natural and right. They were both doing their own thing, living a good life, and I was happy for them.

That Christmas, we invited Orla's family to our house, and we all gathered for a magical, festive time. Beth, my best friend from next door came over with her family too. We played games, ate too much, drank too much and had a wonderful time.

On New Year's Eve, I thanked the universe for these wonderful people I loved, who loved me. For the love story that was me and Tom. For Moira sorting her life out and finally making something of herself. For Frank and his accomplishments, and even Orla, this wonderful young lady who I hoped would become our daughter-in-law.

Life was wonderful.

I didn't notice that I was feeling more tired than usual. I didn't give much thought to the fact I'd lost some weight.

That was my last Christmas, and my last new year's eve.

Sure, life is wonderful. But sometimes, life is also a bitch. And that's a massive understatement.

Chapter Twenty-Five

Marianne

It seemed to take a while for us to get on the road the next day. Apart from the fact we all loved Glencoe and didn't really want to leave, we had Iona's stuff to pack which seemed to have been strewn around every corner of the cottage.

Once every toy, item of clothing and walking boot had made it into Finn's car, we were on our way to Loch Lomond; the last stop in Grandad's journal.

It was totally out of the way for Finn. I offered to go back to Aviemore with him, then visit Loch Lomond on my own, but to my delight he'd said he'd be happy to detour.

I'd spoken to Grandad frequently throughout the trip. I'd emailed photos with descriptions and gave my opinions on the various places. He'd said it felt like he was there with me, and I found myself wishing that he was, sitting on the back seat beside Iona.

I also thought about my grandmother Nora, and how much she must have loved Tom, to leave Scotland. From her little notes in the journal, I could tell she felt connected to this land as strongly as I did. And yet she'd gone with him. That was true love, and the fact she'd died so young, in her 40's was just heart-breaking. Grandad never married again, and I wondered if he'd just never met anyone, or if he'd never got over her loss.

I glanced across at Finn. Complications aside, would I live any-where, to be with him? I caught myself thinking *yes*, felt my panic rise, and swiftly moved my thoughts elsewhere.

I'd decided Inverness would be a good place to live, at first. But once I'd got my business established, I would do a lot of work online, and in theory I could live anywhere. I started pondering the many places we'd visited. The northwest coast was appealing with the gorgeous, quiet beaches... but it was even further to visit my family, or have them come to me. Glencoe was an option; it was one of my favourites and, after a quick google search, a seven-hour drive to my sister's house. Still a day of travel, but not too bad.

There was something about my great-grandparents' farm that was calling to me, if only to visit regularly. Then I thought about the Cairngorms, Aviemore, and Finn's home. My thoughts started to get confusing again, so I suggested we all play a game. It would stop my mind running away with daydreams that could never become reality.

After we'd passed beautiful scenery, played the alphabet game, eye spy *and* talked about our favourite things about Glencoe, Finn pulled up on the shores of Loch Lomond.

We made easy chatter as we got some lunch, browsed the shops, and then booked a boat trip out onto the water.

There was another little girl about Iona's age, and they got talking while we waited beside the loch for the boat to arrive. They were best friends by the time we got onboard, and Iona asked if she could go and sit with her.

As the boat pulled out into the middle of the loch, Finn and I were quiet, looking out at the shoreline and feeling the breeze.

How sad, I thought, I'm on a boat on Loch Lomond with a man I'm crazy about. This should be romantic, but really, it was just depressing. Unable to sit beside him without saying how I felt, I got up, walked towards the front, and leant the railing, taking it all in.

I was there for a little while, contemplating my latest adventures. I'd taken control and made some tough decisions but here I was, about to build a brand-new life. I stood a little taller, feeling empowered for the first time in a long time.

Without speaking, Finn appeared behind me, putting his arms around either side of me to hold on to the railing. He rested his chin on my head, and I leaned back against him a little.

Iona and her friend, an English girl called Leah, were wandering around and I heard them come nearer. I glanced over my shoulder and saw them sit nearby. Finn and I remained quiet, looking out at the view and listening to their chitter-chatter about nothing much. Until...

'Is that your mum and dad?' asked Leah.

'It's my dad,' Iona said. 'That's his friend.'

'Where's your mum?'

'She died. So did my dad, really. That man is really my uncle.'

I felt Finn grow tense, but he didn't move.

'That's sad,' said Leah. 'But it's good your uncle became your new dad.'

'Yes, I'm very lucky. I want him to get married and then I'll have a mum too.'

'Will he marry that lady?'

'I hope so. But he told me they're only friends.'

'They look like they're in love to me.'

They both started giggling, as if this was hilarious, then decided to go and have a look at the rest of the boat.

Rigid, Finn didn't move for several minutes. Then he cleared his throat and pointed to something in the water. 'There's an otter,' he said quietly.

I followed his finger and caught a glimpse for a second, before the otter dipped beneath the water.

'Wow.' I managed to speak.

'She wants a mum,' Finn said quietly.

'It doesn't mean you're not enough for her.'

'I know.'

'Maybe you should join a dating app,' I said. 'Handsome fireman, homeowner, cute kid. You'll have women queuing up.'

The thought made me want to throw up over the side of the boat.

'Let's not talk about my love life,' he said, his voice flat.

'Sorry. Just some advice, as your *friend*.'

'Please stop, Marianne.'

I wanted to ask *stop what*, but I knew. He wanted me to stop reminding him of the terms of our relationship. Truth was, I didn't want to remember them either.

He moved away from me and sat down again. I sat beside him, and we kept quiet for the remainder of the trip.

Iona and Leah parted as if they were long lost soulmates, hugging and promising to email each other via their parents. In a quiet cafe, Finn had arranged a video call with his parents, so I left them to it while I wandered off along the shoreline and called Luna.

We had been texting and leaving voice notes almost every day. Me, sharing my journey, her telling me about the minutiae of her life. I felt I'd known her forever. We shared the same opinions on most things, and although I had many friends back home, I had a feeling she'd be the closest friend I'd ever have.

After catching up on the latest; what was going on in her life and with her children, and me talking about the latest leg of our trip, she asked what my plans were for tomorrow.

'I was thinking, you mentioned you needed some help in the shop...'

She hesitated. 'Oh Marianne, you're hired!'

'Really?'

'Yes!'

'I thought I'd find somewhere temporary to stay. When my divorce and money comes through, I'll buy an apartment or small house, probably in the countryside but within driving distance of Inverness. Then I can work for you and build up my business.'

I'd already told her about my ideas; yoga, spiritual coaching, meditation, mindfulness classes and maybe even organising some relaxing retreats in the highlands. She'd been enthusiastic and supportive, yet challenged me with the right questions and offered to help in any way she could.

'I'm so happy – for you, of course,' she said, and I could hear the warmth in her voice, 'but also for me. I can't wait to have you in my life, in person!'

I laughed. 'Me too. I warn you though, I'm going to be a miserable wreck when I first arrive. I'm on the verge of tears every time I think about leaving Finn.'

She was silent.

'Luna?' I took my phone away from my ear to check it was still connected. 'Are you there?'

'I'm here, I was just thinking about how to respond.'

'Just be honest,' I told her, although I wished she'd sugar-coat it, dip it in chocolate and feed it to me very softly.

'You could live twenty minutes south of my shop and be twenty minutes' drive from Finn. I'm just saying. This is clearly more than a friendship, and I don't get why you wouldn't embrace that.'

I sighed. I didn't want to go into it again, so I made an excuse, promised we'd talk about it when I arrived in a few days, and wrapped up the conversation.

We ate dinner in a cosy Italian restaurant, talking about the day. We'd just finished our dessert when my phone rang. It was Ethan.

'Take it,' Finn said, his face unreadable.

'I really don't want to,' I said, sighing and showing him who was calling.

'You need to sort things out, go on, I'll get the bill.'

'Thank you.'

By the time I got outside, my phone had stopped so I called him back.

'Hi Marianne.'

'Hi Ethan.'

'I'm sorry I hung up on you last time we spoke.'

'It's okay. I know it's a lot to deal with.'

'I had two estate agents over today, I've forwarded you some emails, they think we'll sell quite quickly.'

At last; progress. I didn't realise how much this was hanging over me, and the fact he'd made a step to get us where we needed to be was such a relief.

'Thank you, Ethan, I really appreciate that. I'll have a look.'

'No problem. How's Scotland?'

I looked in through the window at Finn and Iona, they were talking and laughing.

'It's great,' I said. 'It's everything I hoped it'd be, and more.'

'Then I'm pleased for you.'

'Thank you. How're you doing?'

'Good, work is busy. I had a long chat with my sister. Helped me to get things sorted in my head.'

His sister was the only reasonable, level-headed member of his family. I was glad he'd turned to her.

'That's great. For the record, none of this has been easy for me either.'

'Where do you think we went wrong?'

Truth was, I realised with hindsight, we weren't right from the beginning. I just didn't know back then what a good relationship could be. I looked in again at Finn, who glanced at me and gave me a warm smile. I didn't want to hurt Ethan, so I thought carefully about what to say.

'I'm not sure, but you know what, you're an extrovert who loves living in a town, tropical holidays, and sport. I want a peaceful, quiet life, in the country, going for hill walks and reading a good book. We're very different people.'

He sighed. 'When you put it like that... but I won't regret marrying you, Marianne Willow.'

It'd been a while since I'd heard my maiden name. I was happy to hear it again, and it seemed fitting that Ethan should be the first to use it.

'Me either,' I said, realising I meant it. I'd learned so much about myself, and life, and what I did and didn't want. I wouldn't be this person now, this person I was coming to actually like, if it hadn't been for the years with Ethan. I wouldn't be standing here now; everything would be different. So, no regrets.

'Let me know what you think about the house valuations, and we'll get things moving.'

'Thank you, Ethan.'

'All the best, Marianne.' He ended the call. There was something strangely formal about *all the best*, from a man I was married to, had shared my life with, my bed with, for so many years. And yet, all things considered, it felt like we finally had closure.

I waited on the street for Finn and Iona to join me.

'Everything okay?' he asked, his eyes searching mine.

'Yes,' I said, smiling. 'More than okay. Everything's great.'

Our hotel that night was lovely, but of course Finn had a twin room with Iona, and he couldn't leave her there alone. So, for the first time since Aviemore, I went to bed alone. I must admit; I missed him.

Chapter Twenty-Six

Marianne

'Almost home,' Finn said as he indicated off the A9 towards Aviemore. I realised, with a little surprise, that I felt a fizz of pleasure at the thought that this was my home, too, followed by disappointment that it wasn't.

It had been a long drive, and we'd set off early so that Iona could make it to a friend's birthday party. We dropped her off and she made me promise her I'd come with Daddy to collect her in a few hours. I admit, I was looking forward to seeing her again. Until then; I was going to make the most of my time with Finn. I had no intention of seeing him again; it was too complicated. But I didn't need to tell him that. We'd say a goodbye, maybe mention meeting up in future, and then... well, I supposed I'd become less responsive to texts, or send him a polite email telling him we couldn't be friends. I hadn't decided yet.

We moved my bags from his car into mine without speaking or even looking directly at each other.

'Cup of tea?' he asked after we'd dumped his luggage in the hallway. He was staring at the floor, not meeting my eyes.

'Yes please. I'll make it if you like, and you can unpack your stuff.'

He sighed, nodded, picked up Iona's bags and started up the stairs.

I went into his kitchen. I just wanted to leave; this was unbearable. I'd made plans to stay with Luna in Inverness, then I'd start looking for a place to rent and get my stuff moved and set up. I was excited, terrified, full of ideas... so long as I didn't think about Finn, it all felt perfect.

I flicked on the kettle, thinking maybe I should just leave now and get to Luna earlier. I shouldn't have agreed to see Iona later after her party. I could be on my way by now, crying and releasing all this tension instead of pretending everything was fine. It was far from fine. The sooner I got away and moved on, the better.

I realised as I made the tea that I felt worse than ever. So much for Scotland healing me. I'd gone from depressed and anxious to a totally broken heart. I swallowed and took a breath, determined not to let Finn see my emotion.

I was squeezing the tea bags when I heard his voice behind me.

'Marianne.'

I turned. He was a few steps behind me, and his eyes were sad. I couldn't speak, I just smiled. We stared at each other for a moment, and then he was taking me in his arms, kissing me slowly. I wrapped my arms around his neck and kissed him back, savouring every delicious moment; the minty taste of his mouth, the feel of his tongue on mine, the strength of his hands as he gripped me tight.

He pulled away and took my hand, leading me up to his bedroom before he kissed me again. The goodbye looming ahead of us somehow brought more intensity, and every nerve ending in my body felt alight. He took his time exploring my body, and for just a little while I forgot I was leaving. I let go of the pain caused by this man and my feelings for him. Instead, I gave in to the sensation of his body on mine.

Afterwards, he lay on his back, and I put my head on his chest. My heart still thumping and my body buzzing from my orgasm, I put my ear over his heart and listened to it beating. I blinked and my eyes filled with tears, and I watched them fall onto his bare skin. He didn't speak at first, just stroked my hair gently.

'Are you okay?' he said, his voice thick.

'Yes,' I whispered. I wiped my eyes with my wrist.

'We'll see each other again,' he said, squeezing my shoulder.

I nodded. I had no intention of allowing that to happen, it'd be too hard walking away each time. 'I'm going to have a shower if that's okay?' I sat up, facing away from him.

'Of course. Can I get you anything from your car?'

'Just my grey bag, thank you.'

I went to the bathroom, the hot water rushing over me as I let my emotions release and my tears ran down the drain. I hadn't sobbed like this since I was a child. Eventually I peered around the shower curtain and saw that Finn had silently left my bag just inside the door. The lack of words between us was so unusual, it just intensified my misery.

Finn was making us a fresh cup of tea as I drifted down his staircase.

He handed me a mug. 'Come sit down with me for a minute.'

We went through to the living room. It felt so strange, it wasn't that long since we'd been sitting here, but it felt so much longer. I'd seen so much, felt so much, grown so much.

'I'll be forever grateful for this time,' I said, sitting down and sipping my tea and hoping my eyes weren't too red. 'Thank you Finn. You helped me to grow stronger.'

'You did that on your own,' he said, 'give yourself the credit for that.'

'I did, you're right. But I absorbed some of your strength, your steady calmness. You allowed me to open up, to really dig deep and figure out what I want to do next.'

'Well, I'm glad to have been helpful.'

'If the next road trip doesn't come off, then please just know, this has been the best time of my life.'

The words were out, before I could check myself.

'For me, too.' He looked nervous.

I smiled, unsure what to say next.

'Was it better than your honeymoon?' he asked suddenly, then he shook his head. 'Sorry, that's a stupid question, don't answer.'

'Actually, yes,' I admitted. 'My honeymoon was at a crowded hotel in Spain, not my sort of thing at all. Ethan and I barely had any conversation. I realise now we had no deep connection, no emotional intimacy. The initial attraction only got us so far.'

'We have a deep connection.'

'Yep, and the chemistry ain't bad either.' I winked, but he still looked nervous. 'What is it, Finn?'

'I want you to stay,' he said, looking straight at me. 'I don't want you to leave. I want you to move in with me. You can start your business here. Or we'll move wherever you want. Inverness. Lairg. Glencoe. The west coast. Even England, if you want to.'

I held my breath. Wonderful words, from a wonderful man. But. Move in? Be vulnerable again? Become a parent to a five-year-old, overnight? I felt light-headed.

'Finn, it wouldn't work between us.'

'It would, Marianne. It'd be so easy to be together.'

'How well do we even really know each other? We have amazing sex, and we get on well, but Finn, we've never spent time together in the real world - working and taking care of a house - not to mention Iona. How do you see me fitting into her life? You want me to sign up to be a mother as well as your girlfriend, you do realise that?'

'How can you say we don't know each other? We've spent two intense weeks together, twenty-four seven, talking about everything, sharing our innermost thoughts, feelings, secrets. I've never opened up to anyone the way I have with you.'

'Finn-'

'I'm not finished. If you're going to mention Iona, then yes. I have a daughter. She's part of the deal. But I didn't think raising Iona with me would be such a horrific idea.'

'It isn't, I'm sorry.' I felt like shit. I loved Iona, so what was the problem?

'For the record, I'm not asking you to be my wife, or her mother. I was asking you to see what might come next, to create a life together and see what happens. Maybe it'll go well, and we'll form a family. Or maybe it won't, and we'll go our separate ways. Don't you want to find out? Don't you want to try?'

'What about future children?'

'What about them?'

'Finn, I told you I don't want them. I saw your reaction, and you double checked with me on more than one occasion. Every time it's come up, it's clear that it's an issue for you.'

'It is an issue, but not in the way you think.'

'Finn, a life with me means no more kids. No biological children for you. I'm not going to change my mind.'

'A life without you, well that means no more kids, too.'

Eh?

'What do you mean?'

'I can't have kids, Marianne.'

'What?'

'I suffered an injury when I was a teenager, playing rugby. I've always known I'd never have biological children.'

Whoa. A wave of thoughts flooded my brain, making coherent thoughts almost impossible. I didn't know whether to feel sad for him, or mad that he didn't tell me already. Or happy that this meant there'd be no expectation if we were together, which just made me feel like a horrible person.

'So, your reaction on that beach, when I said I didn't want children?'

'I wanted to be sure you meant what you said, because I was already developing feelings for you and if there was any future with us, you'd need to give up any chance of having a baby with me. Naturally, anyway.'

I could hardly believe it. I took a deep breath.

'I'm sorry, Finn. I'm so sorry. You're a wonderful father. No one would know Iona is your niece.'

'Thank you. You don't need to say you're sorry. I knew and accepted it a long time ago, and Iona is a complete blessing to me. I didn't hesitate to adopt her, and I'm happy to be her dad.'

'I know you are, and of course she's a blessing. But, Finn, why didn't you tell me about this when you knew I didn't want a baby?'

'I'm not sure,' he sighed. 'I suppose I needed to know for definite, because if you change your mind in a year, I won't be able to give you that.'

'I won't change my mind.' Everything felt confusing, my mind was spinning. 'But you hinted you wanted more children. You gave me the impression that me not wanting babies was a barrier between us.'

He looked confused. 'When did I hint that I wanted to have a baby?'

Now that he asked, I wasn't sure. 'I don't remember the exact words; I just got that impression from our conversations.'

'I guess whenever you said you didn't want a child, I had two thoughts. One, that we might be a perfect fit, because I wasn't going to be able to have them anyway. I've avoided serious relationships because I know most women want a family.'

'I get that.' Most women did want babies in their happily ever after.

'And two,' he continued, 'despite that, there's Iona. I've already got one. I come as a package deal.'

'And Iona's wonderful, I adore her.' I realised as I said it, that this was completely true. 'But I still can't do this.'

My heart was racing. I couldn't be in love again. It hurt too much when it ended with Ethan. How awful would it be if it ended with Finn, who I already felt more connected to than Ethan and I had ever been? It'd be a million times worse. I'd never recover.

'Marianne, what are you scared of?'

I couldn't answer. But something occurred to me.

'That conversation about kids was near the start of our trip.'

'Yes,' he said, staring at me intently, pain across his face.

'So since then, only a few days in, you've been thinking we might be together, properly be together, beyond this trip?'

He sighed. 'You haven't?'

Of course, I had.

'Yes,' I admitted. 'I thought at the beginning that this would be fun and simple, but nothing about it has been.'

'There's nothing simple about us, Marianne. The pull towards each other, the chemistry, the feelings I have for you, they're not simple. Quite the opposite.'

My chest soared at his words, but I still couldn't do this. This man made me feel a hundred different things I'd promised myself I'd never feel again. And a thousand new things I'd never felt before; stronger, and more intense than I'd ever experienced. To give into this would mean I had a hell of a lot to lose if it ended. I couldn't go back to that dark pit of depression I'd been in, ever again. It was too terrifying. I might not survive.

Finn was staring at me. I needed to get out of this. Out of here. Away from him. I grasped for another excuse.

'Iona...'

'What about her?' he asked sharply, defensive.

'She could get hurt, too.'

'Don't pretend you're worried about her,' his tone was hard. 'You're worried about yourself. You're so scared of repeating past mistakes but Marianne, you and me, we're different. We're meant to be together.'

'Firstly, of course I don't want Iona to get hurt. Of course. And second, yes I'm scared. I have strong feelings for you Finn, but I don't know you that well, not really.'

I could hear the words coming out, hear myself making stupid excuses but I couldn't stay. All I really wanted to do was run.

'We haven't known each other long, Marianne, but this has been an intense getting to know each other. I know we skipped past a few steps, but I know you. And you know me.'

'You don't know me, Finn. You know Holiday Marianne. She's all fun and breezy and adventurous. The real me is boring. I might put on a bunch of weight again. I might get depressed again.'

'I don't care about your weight!' he said, shaking his head. 'You think I care about anything other than you being happy? Us being happy?'

'And if I got depressed again?' The tears started to fall. 'If I got so anxious, I couldn't leave this house?'

'I'd support you. I'd help you get through.'

'You don't know what it'd be like, you haven't had to deal with me when I'm unhappy. Or fat.'

'Marianne, I'll take you exactly as you are. I'm in love with you. And I'll do whatever it takes to help you be happy, and healthy. I'm not going to keep saying this, so for the last time, I don't care about your weight.'

I was holding my breath.

'You love me?'

He moved closer and took my hands.

'Honey, I've been falling in love with you since Stirling Castle, when I saw you talking to Iona. Something deep within me just knew.'

I gasped. 'Finn-'

'Let me finish, please. I've never felt this way before, I've never had the sort of intimacy I have with you. I know we said we'd just be friends, and I thought that'd be fine. I tried to resist my feelings. I also thought it'd be best not to get involved with anyone, because of my infertility and, yes, Iona complicates things. But you don't want kids, and I can't have any.' He was looking at me intently.

'Exactly! I don't want kids, and you have one. I'm not mother material,' I said, my eyes stinging now from all the tears.

'I think you're wonderful with Iona, but you don't have to become her mother. Just a part of her life, a friend if you like. All I'm asking is that we try. You could live somewhere else, if you don't want to move in with us, you could find a place nearby. We don't have to rush into it.'

My heart was racing. I just stared at the floor, my mind a blur of conflicting thoughts.

'Marianne,' he said gently, taking my hand. 'I know this is scary, I'm scared too. But I've witnessed first-hand, time and again, how short life is. We must chase happiness and joy at any opportunity. And we make each other happy.'

'And what if in a few weeks, or a few years, or ten years, we fall out of love, Finn?' I was crying now. 'I can't go through it again. The disappointment, the failure, the loss.'

'I won't ever stop loving you, Marianne,' he said gently, trying to wrap his arms around me.

'You don't know that,' I said, a sob escaping me. I felt the panic rise and I couldn't think straight. I pushed him away. 'I need to leave.'

'What?' he said sharply.

'I need to get out of here. Before Iona gets home. Please tell her... I don't know, just tell her something nice. That it was lovely to meet her and good luck with everything.'

'*Good luck with everything*? Seriously? Come on, you promised her you'd see her later. Please don't leave.'

'I have to.'

'Marianne, please. I'm sorry. Can we talk some more, I'll make us some lunch, we can sit outside perhaps, and talk calmly?'

'I have to go.' I found my bag and flung it over my shoulder.

'I heard you,' he said, standing between me and the front door. 'In the shower. You were sobbing. Perhaps it's arrogant of me, but I think it's because you love me too. You can't stand the thought of leaving any more than I can cope with watching you go.'

I looked into his eyes, watery and sad.

I flashed back to the day I left Ethan, how hard it'd been. This was way harder. If this relationship failed, it'd be even harder if we'd made a life and I'd fallen even deeper for him. When I'd fallen in love with Iona too. Who was I kidding, I already had. This would be a million times worse than Ethan if it went wrong, and I couldn't take that risk.

'Please let me out of here,' I whispered. He raised his eyebrows in disbelief but moved to let me out.

I couldn't stay here, it was too hard, I had to go. I was out the door as quickly as I could, practically flying to my car.

'I really thought you loved me too,' he said softly as I shut the car door, and it nearly broke me to pull off his driveway.

I drove for ten minutes, pulled over and burst into tears. I couldn't breathe and the world started to spin. I almost called him. I imagined my breathless voice begging him to come to me. I pictured him pulling up behind me, getting into my passenger seat and talking me down from the panic.

Breathe in, breathe out. Maybe this time it wasn't a panic attack. Maybe my heart really was going to race to my death. I closed my eyes, feeling like I might black out. After what felt like hours but was only minutes, the panic receded, and my breathing came back to normal.

I let out a final agonising sob and took a deep breath.

Luna. I needed Luna.

Chapter Twenty-Seven

Nora. 1986

Life had its ups and downs. I broke my leg when I was a child. I'd lost my grandparents, parents, other relatives, friends and pets. I'd gone through a few periods of mild depression. I had a difficult pregnancy with Moira, and a difficult time during her *almost-evil* years.

My wonderful Tom and I; we were happy throughout the twenty-six years of marriage but of course we'd had a few rough patches. There were times when we took each other for granted, that sort of thing.

But overall, I had a happy life. Growing up on the farm, meeting Tom, moving to Northampton and then to the Leicestershire village where we raised our kids. Regular trips to visit my family in Scotland. Our courageous, kind, wonderful children were my pride and joy, my everything.

To think I wouldn't meet my grandkids; that I wouldn't get to support Frank and Moira becoming parents. I wouldn't be here to see them grow into middle-age, even. Well, that broke my heart.

Telling Tom about the cancer would be tough, of course. But telling Frank and Moira, that was impossible. When the doctor told me that nothing could be done, that it was too late, too aggressive, too bad... well, I just carried on. I didn't tell a soul.

Of course, they noticed me getting weaker, losing weight, and needing more sleep. I told them I had a thyroid condition. I'd seen something about it on a medical drama on TV, and the symptoms matched up enough for no one to question me. I stopped baking, and they questioned me a little then, but they were all busy and if they were worried, they kept it to themselves.

Frank got engaged to his long-time girlfriend, Orla and I was determined to make it to their wedding, so that kept me going. I realised with great sadness that I'd never know the outcome of their story. I'd be lucky if I saw their first anniversary, let alone meet my first grandchild.

The idea of not existing was incomprehensible; how could you go from having thousands of thoughts and feelings to absolutely nothing? Was there an afterlife? Could I visit these people I loved dearly? Did I have a soul? These thoughts started to consume me.

I had often contemplated the possibility of past lives. I had a friend, back in the Highlands, who practised witchcraft and told me about her past life as a healer on the Isle of Skye, and another life she'd led in ancient Egypt.

I liked that idea; reincarnation seemed more likely to me than heaven or hell. I asked Beth what she thought about it, and she agreed; reincarnation was a thing and she had already decided she was coming back as a man (no periods, no bras, can do whatever you want, she joked).

And so, I spent the next few months after my diagnosis thinking about what my next life might be. Perhaps I'd be a man, for a change. Or even better, a cat. Perhaps I'd be a dolphin or a bird, free to swim or fly wherever I chose. Or a tree. Was a tree possible? Would that be boring, would I even be conscious? Presumably not.

I found books in the local library about reincarnation; I read all I could, learning about all different sorts of ideas and beliefs. Some people believed your soul could choose when, where and who you reincarnated as.

I hoped those people were right, as an idea came to me.

Maybe I could reincarnate as Frank and Orla's future baby. I'd have wonderful parents; and although perhaps ignorant and unaware, my soul would be around my lovely son Frank, and my wonderful Tom would be my grandad. It gave me comfort and took away some of the fear.

Eventually, my family started to worry about my fatigue, and I decided to tell them. It was over a Sunday lunch. Everyone was gathered. I calmly announced it. I said it wouldn't be long before I passed. They were upset and hugged me hard. The look of worry, pain and sadness on their faces was tough. They were mad that I hadn't told them sooner, but I knew I'd done the right thing; I'd spared them that pain for as long as I could.

Tom held me in bed that night and I told him he should meet someone new, after I was gone.

'Never,' was all he said.

I made it to Frank and Orla's wedding, which was wonderful. I had to sit in a wheelchair and be pushed around like an old Granny, (the word Granny made me want to weep, as I'd never be one) but at least I got to see my son get married.

It wasn't long after that.

The family gathered around me, whispering words of love, and gratitude, and peace.

I felt calm as I felt my body giving up on me.

I wished I could have had longer, but I was grateful I'd had a good life. I'd loved deeply and been loved in return. I'd experienced joy. I'd seen my children grow up.

I sent a silent thank you to whoever might be able to hear me for the years I had, and I slipped away.

***

As Nora's eyes closed for the last time, she saw a bright white, silvery light. Her soul lifted up, and she looked down at her weeping family, crowding around the body that used to be hers.

What next, she thought.

Her soul was carried, up and above the Earth, past stars and into the cosmos. She was held there, for a short while, safe and at peace, surrounded by love and light.

In not very much time at all, it was time for her soul to reincarnate.

Nora's soul descended back to Earth, and into the foetus developing in Orla's womb.

Nora's wish came true. And Marianne's existence began.

Chapter Twenty-Eight

Marianne

'Oh, crap look at you, come in, come in.' Luna took one look at my red, puffy eyes and opened her front door wider. 'Callum, we're going to need the living room to ourselves. Fetch wine, two glasses and tissues please.'

Callum, one of the greats, clearly, did as he was told. Soon, we were on the sofa, a large blanket wrapped around us, wine in hand as I told Luna what had happened, sobbing all over her. The fact I still had tears to shed was beyond me. I'd spent the 45-minute drive trying really hard to concentrate as my heart broke and my tears wouldn't stop.

She let me talk, explaining the whole thing, listening with few words to say, and rubbing my back. Eventually, I sat back, downed my wine, and wiped my eyes. A big deep breath and I felt a little better.

'You are crazy,' was all she said.

'I can't allow myself to go ahead with this,' I said. 'I can't explain it, but I just can't.'

'You've been trying to protect yourself from getting your heart broken again. And yet, that protection means you're heartbroken anyway.'

I almost laughed out loud at the irony but responded with only a shrug.

'We need to get to the bottom of this,' she said, taking my glass and topping it up. 'Quick fire answers: why can't you be with Finn?'

'Because he lives in Scotland, and I live... well. I don't even know. Bloody hell, until I find somewhere, I've got nowhere to go but one of my parents, or sisters.'

'Not true, you came here, and you can stay as long as you want. You've got a plan, remember.'

'I bloody love you,' I said, another sob coming out.

'Love you too, sweetheart. Now. Quicker. Why can't you be with Finn?'

'Because I'd be a crap mother to Iona.'

'Why can't you be with Finn?'

'Because the depression might come back, and I can't put that on him. Or Iona.'

'Why can't you be with Finn?'

'Oh God,' I said, realising what I was about to say was so pathetic, so heart-breaking, so raw that I could hardly get the words out.

'Go on. Why?'

'Because I love him, I love him so much. We are so deeply connected, so much more than I was with Ethan and I can't go through that loss again. That pain, falling out of love. Losing something I'd thought I'd have forever.'

'Oh, Marianne. Why else? Come on, why can't you be with Finn?'

'Iona. She deserves so much more than a woman who isn't maternal.'

'We covered Iona. Why else?'

'I don't have anything else.' I sniffed and gulped another mouthful of wine.

'Right,' Luna held up her hand to count off the reasons. 'So, we've got that you don't currently live nearby, that your depression might come back, you think you'd be crap with Iona, and you're scared of getting hurt again.'

She held up her four fingers and I nodded. It felt good to talk, to get it off my chest. Maybe I'd heal from this, move on now. I could focus on me, where I'd like to live, where I could set up my business. I'd get the cat I'd been dreaming of, in fact I'd get several, and never think about being with a man ever again.

Well. Maybe I'd think about Finn when I was alone in bed. I mean, a woman has needs.

Luna held up her index finger.

'One. You love Scotland, so this excuse is null and void,' she said. 'You're going to end up moving here, that much is clear. You've got your plan, or have you forgotten? You feel at home here, you keep saying so.'

'Okay, I concede that one.'

'Two,' she held up another finger. 'Yes, you may get depressed again. But haven't you learned so much in the past few months? You have the tools to get through it. You'd have me, and Finn, and your past experiences. So, I think that one isn't a real reason either.'

I sniffed and sipped more wine.

'Three. Iona. Marianne, I know having a child wasn't on your life plan. But let me tell you this. No one is ever confident about becoming a parent, whether they plan it, or it happens by accident, or they adopt or however that child comes into their life. It's the most challenging, unpredictable job in the world and just when you think you know what you're doing, a new phase or problem comes along, and you have no clue again.'

'You're not convincing me that this is something I want to do.'

'It's also the most rewarding, wonderful experience. But that doesn't mean you have to become a mum overnight just because you're in love with Finn.'

'I know,' I said, taking a deep breath. 'But Iona deserves someone who'll embrace her the way Finn has, who wants to adopt her as their own.'

'Full disclosure; Finn called Callum after you left him earlier today.'

'Oh shit, really?'

'Yes. He figured you might come here, and he wanted us to know a few things. I insisted on the call being on speaker phone. Firstly, he said you were amazing with Iona. And that he hoped you didn't think he was trying to force a mother role on you, because he thought you'd make excellent friends, at least at first. He had no expectations of co-parenting. And, for the record, I could tell by the way you were with my kids, and the way you talk about your nieces and nephews that you're great with children.'

'But I have no maternal instincts.'

'So, you be her friend! But I'm telling you, you do. I've seen you, Finn's seen you. I mean, you're desperate to adopt a cat. That says it all.'

I smiled. 'Iona is just... she's wonderful, Luna. She's bright, and funny and sweet. I suppose I know I'd fall for her like I have Finn and love her with all I have. I just... I don't know if I'd be enough.'

'The girl lost her mother, Marianne. All you'd have to do is show up, be kind, be a positive female role model and she'd be all the better for having you around. So that's another point, wiped off the list.'

I sighed. 'I guess so.' She was making sense, but the fear was still there, raw, and real.

'As for getting hurt again...' She sighed. 'I know it's scary, and there are no guarantees. But you know what else? It's so worth the risk, when you meet that person, the one you're in step with, in tune with... it's beautiful Marianne. There's nothing like it. Don't throw the chance to be blissfully happy away because of fear.'

The tears started to flow again. 'I think I hurt him,' I said quietly.

'He'll forgive you.'

'The fear, it's so real,' I whispered.

'Fear is False Evidence Appearing Real.'

'Ha,' I sniffed. She'd said that to me when I was upset at the Kelpies, which felt like a lifetime ago. 'I've heard that one before.'

'And it's still true. You've no evidence to assume that you'll get hurt again. From what I can tell, Ethan and Finn are completely different people. And you're a different woman than you were when you got married. You're a different woman than you were when I met you at Gretna.'

She was right. Don't you hate admitting it when people are right?

...unless it leads to complete happiness, of course.

'I wish I hadn't drunk all this wine,' I said, hiccupping and sitting up straight.

'Why? Do you have a headache? Shall I ask Callum to fetch us some water?'

'No, no,' I said, holding her hands. 'Because I'd drive back and tell him I'm sorry.'

Luna picked up my phone and handed it to me.

'No,' I said, putting it back on the coffee table. 'It has to be in person.'

Luna picked up her own phone, pressed a few buttons and put it to her ear.

'Who are you calling? Not Finn? Oh please.' I put my hands over my face.

'Hey Finn. Yeah, she's here. She wants to talk, but in person. She's had some wine though.'

I strained to hear his reply but couldn't tell what he was saying.

'Of course. I'll put the kettle on. See you soon.'

Thank you, Universe, for sending me Luna. My new best friend, the woman who knew me so well in only a few weeks. My platonic soul mate. Thank you, thank you, thank you.

Chapter Twenty-Nine

Marianne

Luna helped me to sober up with coffee and splashing water on my face. My eyes were sore, puffy and red. I felt stupid for fleeing, angry with myself. And yet I was excited that he was on his way, relieved I hadn't completely ruined things, that he was willing to come for me.

Finn couldn't get hold of Iona's grandparents, so he arrived at the front door, carrying her as she slept.

He only glanced at me as he carefully laid her down on the sofa. Luna placed a blanket over her gently while I stood there, staring at her gorgeous little face, wondering how anyone, let alone me, could not want to smother this girl with love and affection and help raise her with her amazing father.

I bit my lip as Finn looked at me, his gaze unreadable. I'd hurt him, and he didn't know what to expect.

'It's fairly warm outside,' Luna told us. 'If you want to go outside, there's a bench swing down at the end of the garden.'

Finn gave her a nod and I followed him outside. We walked down the length of the garden in silence, found the swing and sat at either end. Finn stared at the grass, and I had no idea where to begin.

'Hi,' I said, eventually and he looked up at me and smiled.

'I'm sorry I overwhelmed you,' he said. 'I know it was a lot, asking you to move in with me. Telling you I loved you when we haven't known each other that long.'

'No, Finn,' I said, moving to the middle of the swing and taking his hand. 'I'm sorry. I freaked out. I'm so scared of getting hurt again, but also of hurting you, and Iona. Of letting you both down.'

'I get that,' he said, looking down at our hands and then back up at me. 'But I don't think you ever could. You're the most amazing woman I've ever met.'

'Stop,' I said. 'It's my turn to talk.'

He smiled. 'Out with it, then.'

'First, I think us being friends at first allowed me to just relax, I wasn't trying to impress you, I was just being myself. My true, authentic self and I want to thank you for that.'

'Same here,' he said. 'I think that's why it's been so easy being together.'

I nodded.

'What I should have said first,' I said, taking a breath, 'is that I love you too.'

His face lit up, his smile wide and his eyes sparkling.

My voice a little shaky, I continued. 'I was determined not to fall in love with you, but I couldn't stop myself. You taught me to feel again,' I rushed my words, tears forming in my eyes. 'Of course, I want to be together. If you'll still have me.'

A single tear rolled down his right cheek. 'Marianne, I'm completely, utterly in love with you. Of course, I want to be with you.'

He moved closer, putting his arms around me, and I threw my arms around his neck, kissing him hard.

'I can't believe you said you'd move to England for me,' I said, grinning.

'Well,' he said, cupping my chin in his hand. 'Home is where you are.'

My insides soared. 'Well, I want to be in Scotland.'

'Phew,' he said, laughing. 'Want to know something?'

I rested my forehead on his. 'Go on.'

'I was told by Trina, a few months ago. She said I was about to meet the love of my life. And I dismissed it, I thought she was talking nonsense. I didn't think it fair to meet anyone, not with Iona in tow, not with my infertility. And I was still scarred and healing from the trauma at work last year.'

I pulled back to look at him and run my hands through his lovely hair.

'Trina said you'd meet the love of your life. Seriously?' I laughed.

'Yes. And then I met you, and I tried to resist it at first, but she was right.'

Only time would tell if Trina was right about us. But I was ready to believe, and hope, and try, and enjoy the ride in the meantime.

'I love you,' was all I could say.

'I love you too.'

'I've learned so much about myself since I came to Scotland,' I said, sitting back. I wanted to explain, to help him understand how different this was from the last time.

'And when it comes to relationships, I've been thinking... love isn't enough.'

'Explain,' he said, squinting his eyes at me. 'Because this is the first time I've been in love, I have no comparison.'

I tried to find the words.

'Falling in love is one thing. But to build a life together, for it to really work, you need so much more than that. You need shared values, and a similar outlook on the world. Ethan and I were attracted to each other, and then we fell in love. But we never had meaningful conversation, we never discussed what our expectations of each other were. We didn't compare what we wanted life to look like. I'm not sure, if we had, we'd have got married. We had no emotional intimacy. Which is something you and I had from day one.'

He put his hand on my cheek. 'You're right. I've never been able to talk to someone the way I do with you, it's so easy being together. And I know we've been in this holiday bubble, but I want a lifetime with you, Marianne. I want to be with you on the mundane days. For the adventures. For the good and the bad. For it all.'

'Me too,' I smiled, my chest full of fuzzy warmth and joy.

'And I don't have any expectations with you and Iona, to be clear.'

'It's okay,' I said, my tears flowing freely now. 'It'd be an honour to help you raise her'.

And it was.

***

One year later, I was preparing salads for our Summer Solstice celebration. We had just bought a big gas BBQ and Finn was going to cook us up a feast.

My sister Tess and her family were holidaying nearby, so they were due over soon. Luna and her family, too, of course and Trina and her husband, Jed.

'Mari,' Iona said, coming into the kitchen. 'Can I help?'

She was a great little helper, always offering to get involved in the kitchen. I gave her some skewers and chopped vegetables.

'Just be careful with these,' I told her, showing her how to feed the peppers, onion wedges and mushrooms onto the skewers. She sat at the dining table while she did it, chatting away about how much fun she'd had with my nieces Zoe and Clare the day before. I continued preparing salad.

'Are Zoe and Clare my cousins?' she asked, and I turned to face the question head-on. 'Zoe said we are kind of like cousins. Are we?'

'Kind of,' I said.

'When you marry Dad, will you be my aunt or my mum?'

I turned to look at her. 'What makes you think I'll marry your dad? He hasn't asked me.'

'He will,' she said, knowingly, returning to her skewers. 'He told me. But it's a secret.' She dropped a mushroom and put her hands over her mouth. 'Oops.'

I smiled, my heart bursting with love for Finn, and Iona too. 'I promise, I won't tell.'

Mum or Aunt...

Really, it was up to her, wasn't it? Whatever she called me, we'd continue to be the best of friends, and I'd love her all the same. I'd love and support her as best I could.

'What would you prefer me to be?' She put the skewers down and bit her lip.

'I'd like to call you mum.'

'Then, yes, I'd like that too.'

She jumped down from her seat and ran over to me. I crouched down and hugged her. 'I could call you Mum now, maybe,' she said quietly.

'I'd like that,' I said, surprising myself as my eyes got misty. I looked up to see Finn in the doorway, watching us. He mouthed 'love you', his hand on his heart.

You see, the thing is, I didn't want to, or plan to be a parent. But sometimes a child comes along and steals your heart; and they need you. And maybe, just a little, you need them too.

Three hours later, Iona had taken every opportunity to use the word 'Mum'. I wasn't quite used to it yet, but it was growing on me.

I thought about Clara every single day, and encouraged Iona to learn all she could about her, and John too. I would never want to replace the woman who brought her into this world; only do what I could to support and love her with all that I had.

Our family and friends were littered about the garden in a variety of chairs, or relaxing on blankets, eating, drinking, and chatting. I looked around at my new world; the people, the place, the feelings I had. Feelings of bliss, love, contentment, and gratitude – so much gratitude.

After that night at Luna's house, I moved up to Scotland and rented a house about halfway between Aviemore, where Finn and Iona lived, and Inverness, close to Luna. The day my stuff arrived, on a van that'd come all the way from Leicestershire, I wept. I cried again when my piano was set up and ready to use.

I worked part-time with Luna in her shop. My friendship with her was stronger than ever; we talked every day, sharing our lives and supporting each other through the ups and downs of life as they came along. People talk about how hard it is to find a person to fall in love with, but it's just as hard sometimes to find a female friend you really connect and bond with on a deep level. I hadn't realised how much I needed a close friend like Luna, until she came along and filled a void. I was grateful for her every single day.

I started my wellbeing business, and it went really well. I was still taking courses, learning more all the time, and so far I loved what I did. It was starting to make a good profit and, with the magic of the internet, I worked with clients remotely offering coaching, law of attraction, meditation and mindfulness lessons.

I grew a lot spiritually too, eager to learn everything I could from Luna and Trina about moon cycles, crystals, chakras and whatever other topics I could get them to talk about. I felt grounded, connected, and part of something bigger.

After the first six months, Finn suggested again that I move in. I was there all the time anyway, and of course I said yes. The day after I moved in, Iona and I went to a local rescue centre and adopted Glen, our gorgeous black and white cat who we all adored.

Finn had pursued his idea of working outdoors and was now a ranger. He was involved in all sorts, from tracking wildlife to monitoring the weather when tourists might get into danger, to maintaining hiker trails. He loved it, and I'd seen him shift into a slower, more peaceful mindset the longer he worked at it.

It was the most wholesome, grounding, romantic, happy year of my life.

So far.

I blinked. Our little party was coming together. My sister arrived with her little tribe, my nieces running to greet Iona, as I brought a tray of drinks out to the garden. I watched our little group enjoying their afternoon, and my eyes came to rest on Finn. Every time our eyes connected, I felt that flicker of heat, the passion was still going strong. But there was more, too, a deep knowing. He'd just look at me, smile, and I'd know deep in my soul that he was my forever person.

Life is a rollercoaster, and yes, I can't guarantee that I won't suffer depression again. I know that I'll sometimes feel sad for no reason. I will suffer loss, heartbreak, anxiety, and pain. But I will handle it.

So, dear Reader, this is my advice to you:

Surround yourself with wonderful people.

Seek adventure.

Connect to nature.

Don't wait for tomorrow.

Take risks.

And if in doubt; visit Scotland. Every shade of green is awaiting you, and its healing powers are magical.

The End.

~

Thank you so much for reading. If you enjoyed Marianne's story, please leave a review and come chat to the author on social media @iamsarahlsmith or visit sarahlouisesmith.com.
If you feel inspired and would like to travel a similar route then you can find a list of locations visited by Marianne, including photos, at: sarahlouisesmith.com/mariannes-roadtrip

Thank you

Big huge thanks to -

You, Reader, for choosing this book. I hope you enjoyed Marianne's story. If you did, please leave a review, and come message me on social media as I'd love to hear from you.

All of my family and friends who've supported me and encouraged me to write. Massive shout out to Debbie and Zanna, my lovely beta readers for your comments and kind words. And a million thanks to Rose McClelland, my awesome editor, for the fantastic edits, thoughts, and encouragement; this story is all the better for your input.

My wonderful best friend Joanne: I would never have got even halfway through this story without your encouragement, or your friendship which keeps me sane, grounded and smiling on a daily basis x

Chloe, my unconditional love for you helped inspire part of this story. You've taught me so much about motherhood, life and deep bonds that have nothing to do with biology.

Thank you is not nearly enough to express my gratitude to Nathaniel, who encourages me to write, to prioritise myself, and to be the best version of me every single day. I'm honoured to share this life with you.

Sarah x

J&S Romance is a British romance book publisher. We love: female empowerment, strong character arcs, riveting plots, magical chemistry and dashing heroes - who don't rescue our heroines, but rather support and enrich her journey. If you enjoy reading or writing romance, we'd love to hear from you. Follow us on social media @jandsromance or visit our website jandsromance.co.uk

Milton Keynes UK
Ingram Content Group UK Ltd.
UKHW021829210524
443035UK00020B/810